WAYFARING

*Excursions
of the Denim Poets Society*

WAYFARING

Copyright © 2018

ISBN: 978-1-983367-94-6

Publisher's Cataloging-in-Publication

Title: Wayfaring

1. Seacoast literary anthology. 2. Poems, stories, essays. I. Title.

First edition

10 9 8 7 6 5 4 3 2

"'O, Captain! My Captain!' Who knows where that comes from? Anybody. Not a clue? It's from a poem by Walt Whitman about Mr. Abraham Lincoln. Now, in this class you can either call me Mr. Keating, or, if you're slightly more daring, 'O, Captain! My Captain.'"

WAYFARING

Writers of the Seacoast

Managing Editors:

Liz Newman & Roland Goodbody

Piscataqua Press
Portsmouth, New Hampshire

Foreword

This is now our sixth anthology in the Denim Poets Series. As in our first publication, the works contained in the pages here are the fruits of passionate writers aspiring to further learn the craft of expressive writing. Less than a handful have ever published before. This anthology gives voice to their dreams and to their stories.

This book follows the axiom that *most of the expressive potential in our society remains "unvoiced,"* so writes Guy Allen in his collection, *No More Masterpieces: Short Prose by New Writers.*

And so we present to you: *Wayfaring, Stories, Essays & Verse from the Denim Poets Society.*

Our editors believe, as Guy Allen does, that, "There is no good reason why a few should monopolize the pleasure, the power, and the release available through expression.... Given opportunity and support, there are many among us who can create moving, sensitive, funny, shocking, sad, courageous writing."

We wholeheartedly agree.

We hope that the reader of this volume finds much in its pages worth reading.

The Publishers, June, 2018

CONTENTS

KATE JOHNSTON

Author's Note: My childhood home inspired my fictional story "A Forgotten Way." I grew up in a beautiful three-story brick Federal house that reportedly had been a stop on the Underground Railroad. Secret rooms had been discovered; one even contained a chair and a newspaper dated in the 1800s. Evidence of a secret staircase was shown by the outline of steep steps in between two walls, leading up to one of the secret rooms.

This history lured my creative spirit into fantasizing different scenarios involving the old house, the barn, and the pond in the woods. I always wanted to know how the escaped slaves moved on from that sanctuary to their next destination.

I couldn't answer that question to my satisfaction until some characters started telling me their woes. Della has suffered a devastating loss and her grief and guilt are so great she is neglecting her nine-year-old daughter Julia. Chatter from mother and daughter filled my head, but it lacked an anchor. I needed to set them down somewhere, in a definitive time and place, so that their story could unravel properly.

Enter the brick house. It was the perfect setting for the lost, pained souls of Della and Julia. I modified details of the real property for dramatic purposes, but the beautiful and historical spirit remains untouched.

I wrote a post on my blog about my childhood home and how it continues to inspire me today on my writing journey. If you would like to read the post and see a photo of the brick house, please visit *katejohnstonauthor.com/2018/05/25/writing-inspiration*.

Finally, this story is dedicated to my sister Sarah, who would have thought the tunnel was cool, too.

Thank you so much for reading.

A Forgotten Way

DREAD GNAWS AT ME as I enter the driveway of my childhood home, alight with Christmas. My nine-year-old daughter Julia bounces out of the car before I come to a complete stop, my admonishment cut off by the slamming door. She races, hollering, toward the three-story brick Federal house, which had been a stop on the Underground Railroad.

I fiddle with my silk scarf and stare at the old house. The escaped slaves dubbed this haven Pettswood in honor of the name of the people who protected them, Josiah and Anna Petts, and the woods where freedom-seekers waited for the rumbling trains. Over a span of seven years, one hundred fifty-three people had been sheltered in the house, and then helped aboard locomotives heading north to Canada. Here, many lives had been guarded, rescued.

My gut roils.

THE KITCHEN IS WARM AND AROMATIC from the pumpkin and pecan pies baking. Mom greets us with hugs and kisses.

"Are you excited for Santa?" Mom asks Julia.

I shoot Mom a look, but she misses my panic.

"Santa stopped coming after Daddy left," Julia replies. "I didn't make a list."

Mom cups Julia's heart-shaped face with her hands. "In this house, Santa doesn't need a list to know what anyone wants."

I think I see a glimmer of hope or expectation in my daughter's eyes, and I'm stabbed with guilt.

"Your cousins are in the game room," Mom says, and Julia takes off like a gazelle, all legs and purpose.

I kick off my boots into a corner of the coat closet, remove my down parka and squeeze it in among all the other winter gear. Carefully, I place a wrapped package on the topmost shelf.

When I return to the kitchen, Mom says, "Wait till you see Cleo. No bigger than my arm."

My new niece.

Turning my back, I pretend to brush crumbs off the table. "Are they in the game room?"

"No. They're coming tomorrow. Molly's so excited you're here for Christmas, Della."

I ransack the refrigerator for wine. I come up with a bottle. Mom sets two glasses on the counter.

We talk about family news. The fire in the hearth crackles behind me, and I'm swaddled by a degree of comfort until the kids traipse through. Julia is in the lead, holding her combo flashlight and compass.

Her dad gave her this present for Christmas when she stayed with him last weekend. He organized his gifts around a camping theme and included a map of the campground where he'll take her next summer. She hasn't left this gift alone, figuring out her bedroom faces south, and Pettswood is northeast of Draper Mountain. Now it appears she's leading her cousins on some exploration through the old house.

I wanted to object to the tool, because it invited exploration, but what feels worse is the thought of standing between Julia and her dad. I can't bring myself to stoop that low, no matter the fears that seep through the cracks of my foundation.

I watch the children swarm past me and toward the dining

room. Their footfalls echo across hardwood floors warped and dull with age. My memories of the house and the various routes they might take curdle within me. Fifteen rooms, nine with fireplaces. Closets with false walls that reveal narrow staircases, tunnels, and small windowless chambers occupied by chairs, yellowed newspapers and dog-eared books.

My memory clicks over to the door that leads from my dad's office to a path bordered on either side by gigantic wild blackberry bushes. When my siblings and I played our games, this was a favorite route because it allowed us to leave the house unseen and head straight to the old shingled barn that doubled as a pirate's hideout, a dragon's lair or a castle under siege.

Back then, the path was only a meandering foot trail. Narrow, crowded with thorny branches, but we kids liked it that way. Only when we grew up and brought our children here to play did someone in my family—I forget who, and it doesn't matter anymore anyway—decide to cut back the voluminous blackberry bushes and mow a wider path. With over a dozen grandchildren scampering over the property, the idea made sense.

No one knew about the well. A dried-up pit in the earth. Once obscured by the tangled bushes, it didn't reveal itself in true form even after the fortification of branches and thorns had been cut back. A shadow. A soft spot in the soil. A funny area where the grass grew a bit differently. No one investigated. No one worried.

"I should check on the kids," I interrupt my mom.

Her eyes flicker. "The well is filled, Della."

I clamp my lips shut. No one knew about the well, so no one could be at fault. That's what I'm told, a thousand times over, in the pale blue office on Tyntle Street.

"All those secret rooms we found over the years," I say more to myself than to her, yet I want her to hear me. To live with it the way I do. To wake up in the darkest of hours, breathing like you can't breathe. "That collapsed tunnel. What if they get stuck between the walls somewhere, or fall through a false floor..."

"We've been over this house with a fine tooth comb ever since..." Mom's voice breaks, just a bit, a brittle snap like a twig underfoot.

"They know to be careful," she finishes softly.

But the anguish has already filled my hollow center and it's brimming over. "I should unpack."

THE NEXT MORNING, the house rings with joy at the arrival of my sister, her husband, and her four, no, now five, children.

I'm tucked away in my canopy bed, but unstable in the vacuum, the cold space. I grew too accustomed to being cocooned, wrapped snug and warm, from the days I shared the bed with my husband Drew. We managed the three-quarter mattress by curling around each other, legs entwined, his breaths soft above my head. When I close my eyes now he is here. Holding me safe and close. Whispering that we can get through it.

He's the only one who gets it the way I do. And he tried. He tried so, so hard to keep everything going. But I was lost in an endless well of pain, unable to meet his reach.

Squeezing my eyes tight, I try to erase visions of him. I've no right to feel him around me again, like a dream. I gave up dreams when I pushed him away.

I go downstairs to greet my sister and her intact family. Pops of color brighten Molly's fair skin. She's in the midst of handing her baby, Cleo, to our mom, who swoons over her long lashes. I approach Cleo slowly, afraid of what will rise within me. She's slumbering, peaceful. Alive and well. This isn't about me, I remind myself, and I carefully brush my knuckle along her moon of a cheek.

"She's gorgeous," I say and pull back. My sister embraces me, giving me an extra squeeze.

We can get through this. We'll have more, not right away, it's too soon, but someday. We'll heal..." Drew's plaintive pleas ricochet through my memory.

I mumble something about making fresh coffee, and I retreat to the kitchen, acutely aware of the lowered voices in my wake.

THE DAY PASSES SLOWLY, ACHINGLY. Everywhere I turn, someone is smiling or laughing, and I cannot connect with any of it. *Get it over with,* I tell myself. *Just take care of it.* I drain a glass of wine, then go to the closet and fetch my parka. Grinding my feet into snow boots, I grab the package from the shelf.

I walk through the game room to go out the back door. Julia is thumbing through a stack of games. I take in her elongated back, spindly fingers, oversized feet. She'll be tall like Drew.

Julia looks up when she hears me trying to sneak past. "Mom. Guess what Grandma has?" She holds up a deck of cards. "Wanna play Crazy Eights?" An old favorite. My heart swells as the memories hit me.

"Maybe later."

"Do you want to play a different game? Go Fish? We can play for M&Ms. I saw where Grandma hid them," Julia adds, grinning.

"Sorry, I have to do something right now." I edge toward the door.

"Where are you going?"

"Just outside."

"Are you leaving?" Her voice rises a slight notch, and her legs splay like a cat sensing danger.

"No. I need some fresh air. I'll be back." Her posture remains alert. I remember the therapist's advice. I work hard to look her in the eyes and say, "Promise I'll come back."

Outside, the sun is hard on my eyes and the snow is wet and soft. I circle the Federal house to the southern side, where the blackberry bushes are weighted down by heavy snow, like pallbearers struggling beneath a coffin.

The old well is easy to find. The cross my dad made stands tall above the fluffy mounds of snow and beckons me forward. Crouching, I push away snow, scraping at the hardened, older layers until I see cement. There is a heart engraved in the surface along with her initials, Z.F.

I settle into the snow, rolling the package between my hands, watching the engraving blur slowly before me. People tell me I've come a long way, considering, but I still drink myself through the day. Just so I can't picture beautiful things that are no more.

After months of trying to help, Drew let me go. "Della," he said, as he used his entire body to slam the car trunk closed on packed suitcases. A motion too big, too charged with emotion, too unnecessary. "One day, you'll remember what it's like to dream. I *wish* I could be there to see the look on your face."

I watched him drive away. That was two years ago. With the exception of sending Julia to him twice a month and summers, we leave each other alone.

For two months after we separated, I refused to get out of bed. Mornings Julia would get up, make breakfast, and climb upon the bus that waited, chugging, beyond our driveway. She did all this without one word, glance, or kiss from me. I hired babysitters to watch her after school until her bedtime. Some afternoons I couldn't get a babysitter, and Julia was by herself.

Mom discovered I was neglecting my daughter when Julia called, asking what to do about a bloody nose. Mom was at my bedside hours later. Her powerful eyes scrutinized me, reminding me of those owls that roost in the barn.

She ordered me to the window that overlooked the front yard where Julia climbed the twisted pear tree, her fraying braid swinging across her back. "God sent you that little spirit to take care of."

I traced the glass over and over with my fingers. "I failed him once already. What's the point?"

"Because you have a second chance. Right down there."

I'M TRACING THE HEART cut into the cement, over and over, and my finger is bleeding and raw. The snow around me has turned to slush from all my tears and body warmth. Wiping the heels of my hands across my cheeks, I notice the cloud cover and the icy chill in the air. How long have I been out here?

The package rests in my lap. I place it on the cement. Lumpy brown paper secured with a purple ribbon. My whispers are stolen by the rising winds, promises to do better with my second chance. *I must do better. I owe it to the one I have left.*

Laughter and energetic voices cut through my space. I raise my face and look toward the barn, where I see my brothers shoveling a trail through the snow. Looking suspiciously like they are heading toward the duck pond. A trail from the barn to the pond can only mean one thing.

After a final prayer and a kiss on the cross, I continue along the path behind the house and toward the barn. The view of my brothers becomes clearer, and my heart begins a chant. *No no no no no no.* My pace quickens.

Whoever used the barn before our family left behind junk, but amazing junk. Broken horse-drawn carriages, gas lanterns, old-fashioned school desks, mismatched parts of rusty machines, faded scraps of flocked wallpaper, leather-bound books. It is a kids' paradise and for a brief moment I am overcome with a long-lost sense of happiness.

Inside the barn I find my aproned mother pulling down pairs of skates from hooks in the wall. Her grandchildren are scattered around her, trying on different pairs, swapping some for a better fit. My daughter is among them. She's lacing up a pair of worn figure skates that look like they've seen one too many crashes.

"What's going on?" I ask, hearing my voice snag on something deep inside me. My daughter's head pops up, her ocean-blue eyes luminous.

"Look Mom! They fit! They used to be Grandma's."

I hopscotch over my nieces and nephews and peer at her feet. "They look old."

"Yeah, that's the best part. I don't have to break them in or anything. Here, help me up."

She grabs my arm as I stare at my mother. "Where are they skating?"

"The pond."

"The pond? There are thin spots everywhere."

"Uncle Fisher said it's fine."

Amid the flurry of my nieces and nephews I catch Julia's shoulder. "I don't want you to go. I'm sorry. It's not safe."

"Come with us!" my daughter exclaims. "You can make that obstacle course for us like last time. Remember?"

"What I remember is when Tupelo fell through."

"Mom, that was like five years ago..."

"That doesn't mean it can't happen again."

"Tupelo was a dog that couldn't read Dad's sign *stay off pond*," my mother cuts in.

"Yeah!" Julia says. "And this year the ice is much stronger because of all the cold weather we've had."

"I still think it's dangerous..."

"Have Uncle Fisher go out and you watch him," Julia says, her voice quickening. "Have him stomp all over the pond. That'll show you there are no thin spots."

"Great idea!" Mom says. "Your skates are right up here—"

"I don't skate."

"You used to."

"I don't anymore."

"Yeah, like everything else." Tears rush down Julia's face. Her cousins are out the door, hollering down the path.

"Oh Della, take her. You'll have fun."

"Mother, stay out of this. Julia, take those damn skates off. You're not going."

Julia's hands bind in tight fists. "I hate you!"

She rips off the skates and runs to the house. I start to go after her, but Mom stops me with a whip of words.

"Let her go."

"I don't want her alone in that house..."

Mom gives me a funny look. "And you think if you're with her, she'll be any less alone?"

She stomps past me. I stare at the skates thrown behind. The barn echoes with the laughter of the children eager for their skating party, the angry rush and cry of Julia forced to turn in the opposite direction.

The fight with my daughter unhinges me. In my raging fit, I decide to clean out the barn, the one place on the property that's never been razed or updated or fixed.

I don't want the petty job of sweeping. I want to move heavy equipment, rusty tools, junky metal. I want to unload the burdens that made it too filthy to manage.

I find someone else's treasures. A broken sleigh, trunks of moth-eaten clothes, framed photos of strangers, garbage bags filled with military uniforms, old windows and doors. I don't quit for dinner, even though the bare bulbs suspended from the rafters are too dim to work by. From the house, I hear the laughter and the ring of cutlery on china. I wonder if Julia is a part of it. I wonder if she's laughing, or if she's holed up in her room.

Water-stained troughs block me from getting to the back of the barn. I remember when we kids pretended they were open caskets, and we'd lie down inside, hands folded across our chests. If we were the mourners, we'd place wildflowers from the meadow in the dead person's hands. If we were the dead person, we never lay still. We fidgeted, as though to reassure ourselves this was pretend. We were playing dead. Like possums holding Indian paintbrushes.

Those memories are too gruesome to imagine anymore, and I throw my weight against the troughs. With those moved, I'm able to get to a stack of large crates in the back corner. The topmost one is filled with hockey sticks, broken fence posts, scraps of wood.

The box is nailed to the wall. Strange, I think, but this challenge provokes me. I jump down and rummage through tools for a crowbar. Back up the stack I go and pry that crate free with all my might.

It loosens suddenly, and everything teeters and rocks beneath me. I'm falling with that horrible box in my arms. I heave the awkward load to the floor where it cracks like thunder. I crash-land. My head smacks the floor.

Minutes pass before I ease into a sitting position. My back feels bruised and battered, but I don't think I broke anything. I am seeing double, however. The barn spins and tilts, and I feel like I'm Alice in Wonderland. As I pick myself up, my vision fades in and out and I stumble outside.

Snowflakes cascade from the sky. My banged-up body wants to explode and drugs are the first thing on my mind. Sleep, second thing. I don't want anyone to stop me, so I take the servants' entrance, across the galley kitchen gleaming with copper and iron, and trudge up the back staircase. I find painkillers in the cabinet; I don't check the expiration date. I pop two.

THE PAINKILLERS ONLY KNOCK ME OUT for a small while before the pain in my back forces me out of bed. Gingerly, I sit up, noticing my windows are whitewashed with fresh snow.

Downstairs, I pour a glass of wine and wander through the house, the fight with Julia on my mind. I find my sister in the den, nursing Cleo. "Have you seen Julia?"

"She went out to the barn to find you," Molly tells me as she rocks back and forth. Her brows lower. "Didn't you see her?"

There's a blizzard in full swing, so I take a minute to grab my parka and boots. Outside, I'm met by a blinding rush of white like a swarm of angels. The blizzard pushes at me from all directions, and the wind bays like a wolf. The storm is so compact and unyielding I can barely see the barn ahead, a hulking blemish.

Once inside the dry building, I stamp my boots free of snow and call for her. The dim light from the bulbs is barely enough to help me navigate around the mess I left behind.

I slide between the water troughs, watching my footing around the junk on the floor, and head for the staircase to the loft. A two-by-three hole in the wall on my left gapes at me, and I pause. The hole must be a result of rot. Weird thing is that I don't remember this hole from when I was here earlier.

Turning on the flashlight on my phone, I shine it inside

the hole and see a room. Not for storage. It's set up as though someone once stayed there.

"Julia? Honey? It's Mommy. You in there?" No answer. No sound. Not even a whimper.

God. My head whirls a bit and I step back to lean against one of the troughs. I can't stop looking at the gaping hole. I did this. I opened up the hole when I moved the crates.

And here it is, welcoming any curious adventurer like a neon sign.

I grip the edge of the opening. The dark within is scary. Not dark like night, but dark like an empty crib. I climb through.

If I'm impressed with what I discover, then I can only imagine what Julia felt. Tremors and the thrill of adventure. This sight would be enough to keep her exploring and not turn back. But how could she have continued in such eerie quarters?

Her Christmas present from Drew. The combo flashlight and compass. There's no reason she would stop exploring as long as she had that on her.

Artifacts from the 1800s litter this tiny chamber of the Underground Railroad. A cocoon of burlap hangs between the walls, much like ones on a submarine. What used to be food is long gone; all that's left behind are torn pouches and wraps of leather.

A tunnel looms ahead. A small carved-out niche, no bigger than an attic crawlspace, serves as the entrance. The beam of my light doesn't cut enough darkness.

Where does this go? I pause, trying to make sense in my brain made fuzzy by a combination of painkillers, wine and fear. A tunnel. For escape? But to where? Has to exit somewhere, right? Somewhere safe. This had to be how the slaves were moved from the house to their next safe haven. That was over one hundred and fifty years ago. What has happened to this route in that time?

I duck into the tunnel, the image of Julia running away imprinted on my brain. Why did I do this? The dirt closes in. My head brushes the ceiling of the tunnel, and handfuls of dirt shower upon me. The rock and earth smell like mildewed laundry. They taunt me, throwing my calls for Julia back in my face. She was here, now she's gone. If I lose her ... if only I hadn't gone on a mad tear and ripped down those crates. She would be safe.

Just an accident. No one knew about the well. No one knew about the hole. No one's fault. The words play on repeat, but they make no difference. I have lost another child.

The flashlight guides me, yet it also points out beetle carcasses caught in spider webs and scurrying shadows. No. It's my imagination. Keep going. Find Julia.

Pain surges up my spine as I'm forced to walk stoop-backed. The endless dark swallows me step by step. My awkward, painful angle slows my progress and my nerves fray. It means that Julia walked through here twice as fast.

My face brushes through a giant spider web. It sticks to my face and I'm sure something is struggling in my hair. I wig out, tearing at my ponytail, yelling. I stamp my feet and spin around until I'm so dizzy I might faint. Forcing myself to breathe and calm down, I wait for a sensation of crawling anywhere along my body. Nothing happens. I push on, but my flesh is on edge.

The tunnel zigzags like a wild ride. I know why. Granite. A wall of the underground. I keep calling Julia's name. Dead silence responds. Maybe she's already back at the house. I wish that I'll stumble over her, just to find her. What if this is a nightmare brought on by the painkillers?

Every now and then I pause and listen, brush at my whole body, rub my aching back. How far does this thing go? Why haven't I found her yet?

Something in the dark is watching me. I hear it coming up from behind. I run, even as I know I'm being terrorized by my imagination.

The tunnel angles upward, and I climb, tearing through cold earth, stones, and worms. Roots yank my hair and scrape my face. I have to shut my eyes and hold my breath as I push through dirt, rocks and dead things.

I emerge through a hole in the ground. Hesitating, I realize I've come up into some sort of a cave. The entrance is partially covered with vines and debris. Beyond, nothing but billowing snow and trees. Hibernating animals are on my mind, but so is Julia. I haul myself out of the hole and look around, waiting for my eyes to adjust to the filtered light.

A mound in the corner catches my attention. Swallowing with nervousness, I shine my light over the lump and recognize my daughter.

"Julia." My voice is filled with a combination of relief and apprehension. I rush to her inert form and shake her. "Julia?" Is she ... ? I shake her more aggressively.

Her body jerks slightly, and her eyes pop open. I lean back to get in her line of vision. "Julia! It's Mom."

Her mouth shakes. "Mommy?"

She sits up and throws her arms around me, sobs spilling onto my shoulder. "Mommy. Mommy." We hold each other the tightest I can ever remember. Pulling back slightly, I check her over. Her cheeks and forehead are scraped raw and bleeding. Her hair is filled with dirt, leaves and twigs. She is dressed only in jeans, sneakers, and a light sweater.

"Good grief, Julia, you're freezing." I strip off my parka and boots, and stuff her into them as quickly as I can. Her teeth chatter.

"What were you doing?" I ask, rubbing her back and arms vigorously. She burrows her face into my shoulder, and I can feel her icy breath through my shirt.

"Looking for you," she says through clattering jaws. "I thought you were in the barn."

"I got hurt. I went up to my room." I pull back to examine her again. Her face is bleeding and puffy. I think snow will help the swelling, but I want to warm her up first. I pick the debris out of her hair, finding a couple of dead spiders, but I don't mention it.

"I'm sorry. I know I'm not supposed to go into places like that without a grownup." She tilts her face up at me. "But when

I saw that room, I thought that's where you were. 'Cause you like old stuff."

I release a small laugh.

"Then I saw the tunnel."

"And of course you had to check that out." I let out a sigh. "You know not to go into tunnels or anything like them!"

"I didn't think it would really go anywhere..."

"Do you realize what could have happened?"

"It just looked so cool." She leans away from me, and I feel a draft. Tears drop from her eyes and roll along the scrapes on her face. She's here, safe. Don't lose her again.

I take her hands in mine and rub them vigorously. "It did look cool, actually. You were really smart to stay in the cave. I know you could have kept going, especially because you have that compass. But you didn't. You stayed put." I blow my warm breath on her fingers. "That was really smart of you."

Julia's response is to look out the cave entrance. "If it wasn't snowing, I'd have tried to get back to the house."

"Now, Julia, why in the..." I slam down on the automatic feed of admonishment in my head. I lift my chin. "I bet you would have found your way back. No problem."

The tiniest hint of a smile touches her lips, and my heart pulses with lightness.

"Where are we anyway?" she asks.

"Remember how Grandma told you stories about the escaped slaves hiding in the house?"

"Yeah."

"I think this might be another hiding spot. Where they waited for the train to help them go on to Canada."

"They took the tunnel to get here." A frown creases her brow. "So this is a safe place."

Warmth and regret fill me at the same time. "This is a safe place," I repeat and hold her warm and snug against me.

IT'S TWO IN THE MORNING when I stir Julia awake. She mumbles, smacks her mouth in thirst and pushes at me.

"Open your eyes, Julia. Santa came."

"No, he didn't."

"Yes, he did. Get dressed. Come see."

I lead the way to the pond. The sky is tangled up in stars. The moon sways over Pettswood, shining on the ice where my brothers had cleared away the snow from the afternoon's blizzard.

Julia and I approach the edge of the pond where our skates rest. "What are we doing?" Julia's voice is a hush.

"Skating," I say.

Her eyes are wondrous. I double-check the knots in her laces. We step on the ice. I kiss Julia on the head. "Merry Christmas," I say and swoop her in a wide circle. She squeals with glee and takes off on her own. Ice skating is branded on her. She hasn't forgotten even when her mother thinks forgetting would make things easier.

I take to the ice, baby steps at first, and then longer strides, until I'm gliding right behind her. The stream of moonlight follows us. I tilt my face up. I'm sure I see the arc of sleigh tracks along the grid of stars.

ROLAND GOODBODY

Author's Note: Parted in the Middle is one of a series of essays about family and personal identity. It describes a brief idyllic interval in my life that, in the light of subsequent events, came to feel like something of a cruel irony. The disjunction has prompted me, over the course of time, to examine the influence on our lives of the circumstances in which my siblings and I grew up. Two accompanying photos—one of the abandoned house and its garden, and the other, of my two brothers standing in front of a giant rhubarb plant (or *gunnera manicata*, to give it its scientific name)—may be viewed at *rolandgoodbody.wordpress.com*

Parted in the Middle

IT WAS THE MOST UN-BRITISH OF SUMMERS. The period from June to August of 1976 saw the hottest average summer temperature in the UK since records had begun over 350 years before, and this, combined with the severe year-long drought, etched it permanently in the national psyche. Close your eyes and you could have imagined you were in the Mediterranean. "No point forking out money going to the Riviera this year," people said, "The Riviera's come to us!" Others quipped that such settled weather was more than a little unsettling. The jokes dried up, however, the longer the heat continued. By midsummer, everyone was moving as if mesmerized, sleepwalking their way through the days.

There were extraordinary sights. An extended heatwave, a run of fifteen consecutive days with over 90-degree heat, prompted factories all over the country to limit production to morning shifts in order to minimize the risk of heat exhaustion. Entire workforces could be seen clocking on at 4am and wearily making their way home to darkened afternoon bedrooms. The lake in our hometown, all twenty-two acres of it, was reduced to little more than an oversized puddle, its bed parched and riven with deep cracks, a sight no one had previously beheld nor ever expected to see again in their lifetime.

For six weeks of that summer I stayed with two of my brothers—there were five of us in all, all boys, and I was the eldest—in a house on the edge of the village where I had been born. They had already lived there for many months, but I was just returning from a spell teaching English at a tiny secretarial school in northern Spain prior to starting graduate school in the United States in the autumn. For me, it was an interval between foreign travels, a chance to catch my breath and to take stock, a respite in which to prepare myself mentally and emotionally for the next chapter of my life.

My time in Spain had been difficult. I'd arrived with no teaching experience and no knowledge of Spanish or Spain, and for the first few months I was completely out of my depth, alone with no one to confide in. Yet when the time came to leave, I had fallen so much in love with the country that I was deeply torn between staying and going. In the end, I took the path of least resistance and allowed the forward momentum of things already set in motion to carry me. But when the day of my departure came, I was heart-heavy and felt as if I was leaving a part of myself behind. The feeling stayed with me throughout the voyage home. As the ship sailed past Finistère in Brittany, I peered into the dense coastal fog towards the island of Ushant hoping to catch a glimpse of someone who lived at the desolate end of the world, someone who might know how I felt.

I was glad the crossing took thirty hours because it allowed me to reconcile myself to the choice I'd made. By the time I disembarked in Southampton, my spirits had improved, and I took the broad morning sunlight as a good sign.

The house my brothers and I lived in was a conventional two-up, two-down terrace. It had a small but neat back garden and an even smaller patch in front, which gave out directly onto the street. Across the road stood open woods, save for a few houses hidden behind a long, high privet hedge. The closest of them was abandoned—it had been owned by a doctor, my brothers told me, who had gone through a messy divorce that had left him bankrupt. It sat on an acre of land, with a large, overgrown garden in back extending all the way down to a stream, alongside which ran a footpath that led to a larger village and the train that took us to the nearby town.

Each weekday morning after my brothers left for work, I lingered in bed, soaking up the early sunlight streaming in through the window and luxuriating in my freedom, relishing the notion that I had the whole day to do whatever I wanted. I slept in a workroom in a narrow single cot and woke to the smell of fresh lumber stacked on the floor. A few floorboards were missing and there was no door, but I liked the room's sparseness and its unfinished quality. Once up, I'd move slowly through my day, either sitting in the living room listening to cricket commentary on the radio while writing in my journal or relaxing in the garden reading, or perhaps taking a long walk along country lanes, returning in time to have dinner with my brothers.

The three of us rubbed along well that summer, bent on making a go of functioning as a tiny family unit. Back in the depths of winter, the three of us had spent a few nights sleeping

---

rough when our dad had turfed us out of the house. I had then returned to Spain and they had been fortunate enough to borrow the house from a friend, but we were all aware of the hardship we might be forced to endure if things didn't work out. So, I was pleased to see that Clive and Trevor seemed to be getting along. They had never liked each other very much and were as different as chalk and cheese, the one surly, the other idealistic. When I asked Trevor about this rapprochement, he said, "Oh, Clive's not too bad as long as you don't get him started." This was quite a change from his having nicknamed Clive *Aspirin*: "because you bloody well need one after you've been with him"—so things were looking up. We made our own entertainment that summer—we had no television—and joined in each other's activities, even when we had no real interest. For instance, Clive didn't much like football, but he threw himself into the little games we played at the recreation park, while I, for my part, accommodated to their love of snooker.

Once a week, the three of us would cut through the garden of the abandoned house and follow the footpath along the stream to the railway station to take the train into town. On one occasion, we stopped to look inside, carefully entering through the unlocked French doors in back. Although it was in a state of dereliction, the house was striking. It had white painted stucco walls instead of the usual brick, and boasted an enclosed wooden verandah painted sky blue in the rear, which combined with the wildness of the garden, created the impression of its being an exotic African plantation house.

My brothers had already seen inside it and quickly lost interest, but I was keen to explore everything. While Clive went out to the garden to wait, Trevor hovered, I remember, curious about my enthusiasm.

On the floor in the middle of what once must have been the office were a few discarded items—books misshapen by dampness and mold, old bills, broken shelving, the flotsam and jetsam of a life. I would have stayed longer to savor the desolation of the deserted rooms, hopeful always of finding something totemic to salvage, but I could tell Trevor wanted to be on the move. There was, in any case, little of genuine interest, except for a slim green paperback Baedeker travel guide of Germany and the Alps, which I pocketed. When I turned to tell Trevor that I was ready to go, I discovered that he'd already left.

I FOUND THEM BOTH at the bottom of the garden looking at a giant rhubarb plant. It was so extraordinary that I asked them to pose in front of it and took a photo of them. In it, they look as if they are standing in a jungle, the weeds and wild grass coming up to their waists. Trevor is gently clowning, pulling a face as if he has just seen something crawling towards him through the undergrowth. Clive has taken hold of one of the large leaves and is turned slightly sideways, as if indicating to a television audience something about this particular species of plant. His hair is neatly parted on one side, while Trevor's, only recently shorn of its flowing blonde locks, is parted in the middle. Many weeks later, three thousand miles away, I pinned this photo on the wall of my small office as a gesture towards family and home. Alone in strange surroundings, it seemed important to have something from a place and a time that was familiar.

The weeks passed and summer drifted towards its conclusion, while I mentally started to prepare myself for the next challenge.

Towards the end of our time together, Trevor and I spent a few days at the Cambridge Folk Festival, hitchhiking the hundred or so miles back to the village by way of London. I found us a cheap café near Foyle's bookshop in the center where we ate lunch and I remember Trev seemed impressed by my familiarity with the city.

After lunch, we made our way to Wimbledon Common and picked up the A3, the main road south, where we stuck out our thumbs again and got back to the village of Rake, a few miles from home, in the early evening.

"How about a pint before we walk back?" Trev suggested.

Small pleasures like this were something we rarely allowed

ourselves. Growing up poor had prejudiced us against frittering away what little cash we had on such luxuries. But it had been a remarkably good day spent together and it warranted a modest celebration. For once, I had felt like the older brother I was. So, we got our pints and sat outside at a picnic table, relaxing companionably in the waning sunlight, eating a sandwich and sipping our drinks. We were easy together, chatting leisurely, smoking a cigarette in the summer warmth. As the sun started its descent, I noticed the way the light fell on Trevor's hair, how his nostrils flared when he spoke.

We strolled back to our village, two miles distant, along a winding lane bordered by high hedges. After a while, Trev asked if I'd noticed the column of ants that was marching along the bank beside us. I hadn't. He pointed them out to me and said he'd been tracking them for a while. I asked how he'd noticed them.

"Oh, I saw a few stragglers a mile back and just put two and two together. I thought we'd find the column eventually."

I had never seen a column of marching ants before. I'd also never seen this side of Trev—his curiosity about the natural world, his patient observation, and a shy competence about him that was entirely new to me. I watched him out of the corner of my eye with wonderment, thinking how little I really knew him, that I didn't quite have the measure of him that I'd thought. As we walked on, I mused on how much time I'd spent away from home, either at university or abroad, missing these changes in him and in my other brothers—and then ruefully reflected that I'd be doing precisely the same thing again soon enough. I realized then that our time together was something precious, to be savored, and I didn't want the walk home to end. In that moment, I could have stayed with my brothers for many more months, sharing our days cocooned away from the world, "lightfoot in heart's ease and school-free" (in David Jones's phrase), one day merging seamlessly into the next, ensconced in a time unmeasured by the clock.

But it was not to be, and, as it turned out, that evening

walk along the country lane was the last time Trevor and I were close, never afterwards managing to repeat its intimacy. Instead, we had petty misunderstandings, blown out of all proportion by mutual mistrust. Looking back, I'm sure our occasional closeness could only have increased for him the pain of the distance I more often kept, not out of any hostility towards him, but simply because of where my life took me. After graduate school, I stayed in America, got married and settled down. My visits home to England were infrequent and relatively short, so our time together was limited. In 1979-80, I spent eight months there with my wife, to be closer to my family, but rather than it be the occasion for Trevor and me to renew our friendship, it was the year we fell out. One spring afternoon, I lost my temper with him because he unapologetically showed up hours late for a planned get-together between us for which I had rearranged my work schedule. When he arrived, I was raking leaves on the grounds of the large estate where my wife and I were a live-in couple. I told him I couldn't take any more time off and I was annoyed that he expected me just to drop my tools to be with him.

"I got in a long, drawn-out argument with the old man, didn't I? I couldn't get away any sooner."

"Seems like every time you go over there, you end up arguing with him. It's like a bloody routine, a ritual you've got between the two of you."

"Well, you know what it's like arguing with the old man," he said. "You more than anyone ought to know. He never admits to being wrong, even when he's proved to be. He'll swear up one side and down the other that he never said it. It's bloody maddening."

"You're quite right, I *do* know, which is why I don't engage in arguments with him any longer. So, why do you go there, especially when you've got other commitments? It's a choice you make yourself. You know what's going to happen. You told me that you'd be here three hours ago."

I was unforgiving, and eventually he stormed off in a huff and

I didn't try to stop him, thinking that, as his older brother, it was time I taught him about responsibility and consideration for others. It must have felt to him like a betrayal of sorts. Consequently, whenever we saw each other, he was distant with me, when once I had been his hero. Later that summer, he got married and soon became a father, and no longer had time for me.

FIVE YEARS LATER, I got a phone call at my apartment in New Hampshire after shopping at the A&P on my way home from work.

It was Dad. He seemed to be buoyant, and I remember that we talked about the weather for a bit. Then he asked if I was sitting down, and I said, "Yeah. As a matter of fact, I'm sitting on the floor. Why?"

"That's good, 'cos I've got some bad news for you."

"Oh yeah, what's that, then?" I said. I thought it was a joke because of the way he said it. But he didn't answer me; he just made a sort of strangled sound in his throat. And then there was silence.

Ralph came on the line. "Hello, Roland."

"Ralph, what's going on? Is the old man okay? One minute he's talking to me and the next he just walks off and leaves the phone. Is he drunk?"

"No, he's not drunk."

"Well, what's happening then? He said he had some bad news to tell me. Do you know what it was?"

"Look, I'll put Mark on, alright?"

And then Mark says, "Hello, where've you been? We've been trying to call you for hours. You been out on the town again?"

"No, I haven't been out on the town! It's only about six o'clock here, isn't it? I've just done a bit of shopping. Look, what the hell is going on there? First Dad's on the phone, then Ralph, and now you. What's this about some bad news he was trying to tell me? Do *you* know?"

"Yeah," he said. And then he choked a little, "Trevor's dead."

I still have the receipt from the A&P.

I FLEW HOME FOR THE FUNERAL. The day after I arrived, we went to the undertaker's, although I wasn't exactly sure why because no one had told me the purpose of our visit. I assumed we were going to choose a coffin. We sat in silence in the waiting-room. Dust motes floated in the beams of sunlight that slanted in through the window and flooded the plastered-over fireplace. Eventually, we were led across the street, through an arch and down an alleyway to another building. It began to sprinkle with rain. Rock music played faintly in the flat above. Ahead of me, my mother supported my grandmother on her arm, followed by the rest of the family.

We entered what looked like a converted stable and I heard a sudden large intake of breath and then my mother quietly began to moan. I thought it must be the sight of all the coffins. So, when my eyes adjusted to the darkness, I was totally unprepared for what I saw—my brother Trevor lying embalmed in his coffin.

His hair was parted differently, and it made him look unlike himself. I noticed that the flesh around his neck lay in thick folds. Later, I asked my youngest brother if Trevor had been drinking so hard towards the end that he had put on a lot of weight. "No, that's just the way your neck looks when your muscles let go, innit?"

I stood there looking at him, wanting to be brave enough to follow the example of my mother and grandmother and bend down to kiss him goodbye, but I couldn't bring myself to do it.

At the funeral, the four brothers carried the coffin; being so much shorter than the others I found it hard to hold up my end, and my youngest brother ahead of me bore the brunt of the weight. I heard his labored breathing and muttered protests as we walked up the church path and into the church: "I can't handle this...it's too heavy."

Dropping the coffin became a real possibility, but it was unthinkable, and it took all our resolve to keep it aloft. Beads of sweat popped out on my forehead. After a great deal of effort, we made it to the altar and managed to lay the coffin down and once we'd taken our seats in the pews, the ceremony began. Sitting there, I was chagrined to realize that I had been so preoccupied with the task of carrying the coffin that I'd become oblivious to its contents.

THERE'S A PHOTOGRAPH OF US taken at the wake in which we're lined up against a brick wall in rented suits and black ties, unsmilingly squinting into the sun at the camera, looking like suspects in a line-up or hostages about to be shot.

I KNEW THAT TREVOR HAD RECENTLY SPLIT UP with his wife, but living on another continent, in the era before cell phones, e-mail or internet, I didn't know any details and I was in the dark about how he was coping. My own marriage had broken down only a few months earlier and I was distraught. I had naively assumed that everything would work out in the long run for both of us, that we'd get through our separate upheavals. It turned out that his wife had kicked him out of the marital home after he had admitted to having an affair with another woman and she wanted a divorce. It was unlikely he'd be allowed access to their two young children, a four-year-old girl and a twenty-one-month-old boy.

He had moved back in with our parents. Apparently, on the night he killed himself, he'd gone out for a drink with a friend and was later laughing and joking at home. But after everyone else had gone to bed, he'd slipped out of the house and driven to a remote country lane where he'd attached a length of hosepipe to his car exhaust, threaded it through the rear window and switched on the ignition. According to my youngest brother, Trevor had bought the hosepipe a few weeks earlier at the local hardware store. Deciding to end it must have given him a measure of relief and would account for his light spirits, which had fooled everyone into thinking he was coping with the situation. He was 28.

OF THE FIVE BROTHERS, Trevor and I were the most alike temperamentally. Outgoing, though sometimes moody and hard to read, we were sensitive and easily slighted, and both of us were looking for something more from life. As the one who first left home for a place of his own, and who then went on to university and abroad, I was an example for Trevor, someone he looked up to. When he made various attempts to leave home himself, it was only natural for him to expect me to be supportive, which I was, but our relationship never developed into the kind of nurturing brotherly love that would have benefitted both of us.

Despite having grown up together in a small house, where we were constantly in each other's company, and even slept in the same room, my brothers and I weren't especially close as siblings and never forged strong brotherly bonds. Rather than uniting us against a common foe, our father's alcoholic moods and frequent cruelty had the effect of splintering our relationships, so that each of us sought our own singular path toward self-preservation. Confidences were rare, trust in each other even more so. Consequently, we formed only shifting alliances and fugitive attachments, always strategic and provisional. Perhaps not surprisingly, then, as adults we were cagey with each other.

Growing up being physically and emotionally abused—even in a time when hitting your kids wasn't seen as aberrant behavior—inflicts lasting psychic damage. It knocks the stuffing out of you, riddles you with self-doubt, deadens you, and it can seal you off from really connecting with others. My relationship with my brothers was collateral damage.

Could I have been a better brother to Trevor? There are certainly things I wish I had done, such as taken a greater interest in him, been more available to him, and, at the end, made more of an effort to patch things up between us. But I've never been in any doubt that it was our upbringing that was principally to blame because we were so limited in how much we could reach out to each other. I hardly knew how to take care of myself, much less minister to my brother. It's not guilt I feel, it's sadness. Sadness for what was lost—most achingly, my brother, but also, and earlier, brotherhood itself.

So, for me, the summer of 1976—when we were thrown together by circumstance outside the family home and slowly began to feel our way towards each other, like plants seeking the warmth of the sun—will always be the high watermark of our time together as brothers, memorialized in the photograph I took of Clive and Trevor in front of the wild rhubarb plant. That photo, now a cherished possession far more precious to me than the long ago lost Baedeker I rescued from the abandoned house, captures a moment in time when everything was there— the pleasure in each other's company, the shared humor, the elusive bond tying us together.

Looking at it now, I see again with pleasure the pleasure in my brothers' eyes, the unspoken assent that at least for this short passage of time we are walking the path together.

WOODY SPONAUGLE

Author's Note: This a story about becoming a target for retaliation after challenging fraud and misrepresentations, and its cost to a reputation and demand on family resources, financial and otherwise.

It is an early chapter in a collection of stories that recounts a key turning point in my life where I went from a cell, metaphorically 'the lowest form of sustainable life,' to some accomplishment in the space of a few years. It started a chain of experiences that dramatically influenced the future of our whole family. The purpose of the stories is to refresh the memories of family members and enable them to add their own recollections of the events and fill in some gaps.

Presumably there are some lessons that may be of value to my grandchildren. If nothing else, they may provide everyone with a lot of laughs.

I would like to think that I have repaid, in some way, all of those in this story who helped during this ordeal.

The Arrest

"FIND PUTTRA," I instructed Mina, "and tell him where I am going."

Those were my last words as I left my office with the two Thai police officers who had demanded I accompany them to the police station. The policemen refused to say why I had to go with them, but I couldn't very well resist. If I did, there would be handcuffs and possibly a pulled gun. Besides, the Lumpini police station was just ten minutes away on Wireless Road beyond the US Embassy in Bangkok. Despite the seriousness of the police appearing at my office, I felt sure that after answering a few questions or providing a statement, I would be able to return to my office. I was to discover that my confidence was misplaced.

The Lumpini police station, a one-story building on a raised wooden platform, was primarily a holding station for suspects not yet formally charged and who could not afford their fines or post bail. The station's entrance opened onto a large room with several policemen milling around and processing tables and desks covered with piles of paper. A typical Thai government office, with no air conditioning, just ceiling fans slowly pushing the warm air. Several officials moved around lackadaisically to avoid sweating, a trait mastered by those living in the tropics. A few others tried unsuccessfully to hide their curiosity about the large farang, the Thai name for foreigners. Namely me.

INCARCERATION

"Sit," ordered the officer with a pencil-thin mustache, pointing to a chair. From the Captain's bars on his neatly pressed uniform and his commanding tone, I assumed he was the station chief.

Although he was no doubt familiar with the case, the intensity of his focus while leafing through the thin file in front of him was designed to intimidate. He broke his silence by advising me in cryptic English that they suspected me of theft.

"Theft of what?" I asked.

"Equipment," he responded.

"What equipment? Theft from whom?" I asked.

"From your company."

My company? Was he saying I had stolen something from myself? Even allowing for poor English, this remark made no sense.

"Put your wallet here," he said, pointing to a paper bag.

"Your watch, too. And empty your pockets," he ordered.

When he did not ask me any questions about the case or if I had any statement to make, I quickly realized he was processing me for incarceration! I needed Puttra now to get here to stop this before it goes further and clear up this misunderstanding.

"Can we wait a few minutes until my friend gets here?"

"No."

"Can I make a phone call?"

"No."

Putting the bag with my possessions in a drawer, he called over another officer, gave him some instructions, and then stood.

"Go with him," he directed, pointing to the other officer.

Having no choice, I rose, and the officer led me across the floor, around a yard-high slotted iron rail, and into the cell block. He turned to the first cell on the left, opened the door, and gestured for me to enter.

When I entered the cell, he loudly slammed the door shut and turned the key.

My Cell

THE CELL BLOCK HAD TWO ROWS of cells with a large and small cell in each row. None of the cells had any furniture, just well-worn smooth teak floors. Along the far wall in each cell was the Asian style toilet, a two-foot-wide raised concrete trough with a water faucet at one end and a drain hole at the other. A dented metal bucket sat in the trough and its use became clear when they turned the water on for only one hour twice a day. I soon discovered that I had to bathe immediately when the water started so I could then refill the bucket to wash down the trough after toileting.

The police station was situated between an upscale residential part of Bangkok and the notorious Patpong nightclub district, making its prisoners a curious cross-section of Bangkok nightlife. Most of the prisoners were brought into the station in the evening, usually for drunkenness, fighting, drugs or some other petty offense. They would spend the night sobering up and typically be released the following day after paying their fines or posting bail. The number of occupants in the bullpen ranged between ten to twenty men at any one time.

Initially, having seen the small cell opposite me occupied by an assortment of prostitutes, identifiable by their miniskirts, makeup, and boots, I assumed the small cells were for women. But then a non-English speaking male foreigner was moved from the bullpen when the private cell became vacant. Later, a fight victim was put into the small cell to separate him from his assailants in the bullpen. This move did not stop their arguments that continued throughout the day and into the night. Then, when a couple of times multiple occupants were put in the small cell for some unknown reason, I became concerned. Would I be forced to share my cell? It was barely large enough for me alone; if I had a cellmate, it would be even more uncomfortable.

THE THAI WAY

I had been in Thailand long enough to know that things moved slowly, and often in unexpected ways. You were more likely to get what you wanted or be more successful by adapting to the 'Thai Way,' showing respect rather than becoming loud and obnoxious when frustrated. Experience taught me that being patient and polite even in this abusive situation would be more rewarding than being an "Ugly American." I fought to remain calm and not let any anxiety and especially panic show, both of which would have only made the situation worse.

Later in the afternoon, I could see, but not speak with, my wife Judy and Puttra, who had finally arrived. As they talked with the police, they turned and looked my way every so often and smiled as though to reassure me, but their mostly worried looks told me their conversations were not going well.

Why are they having problems?

Don't they know this is the second time I have been set up? This is all part of a pattern!

But then additional thoughts crept into my mind.

Are Andrews' charges more serious than the last time?

Has Pradian rigged the system, making it harder to overcome?

Who have they paid this time?

At last, the visiting hour began. But it was unlike anything I expected. Private conversations were impossible. Judy, Puttra, and my lawyer Preecha, who had just arrived, joined the crowd bunched up together behind the rail outside the cell block doors a few yards away from the cells. There were ten to twenty or more people at any one-time jostling for space along the rail to talk and more often shout simultaneously across the gap. Wives and girlfriends harangued their husbands and boyfriends for being drunk and getting thrown in jail. Women with children in their arms were upset having to pay their husbands' fines for their release. Adding to the marketplace atmosphere, relatives and friends of those who could not be released would hand food, drinks, clothes, and towels through the bars to the guard to pass to the prisoners.

After squeezing through the crowd, Judy and a few friends took turns handing me mosquito spray, some food, a toothbrush and toothpaste, pen and paper and most importantly, bags of fresh water. Water, and later soft drinks, were delivered Thai street vendor style - in a plastic bag with a rubber band wrapped around the inserted straw. Despite the heat, I had refrained from drinking out of the faucet fearing diarrhea.

"You'll probably need this," Judy said, handing me a pakama. Having used the traditional all-purpose Thai cloth upcountry, I knew she was right. While the other prisoners used their pakamas as loincloths, mine became my bath towel, floor covering, and blanket.

ALONE

After the last visitors left, the station became quiet and my world shrank to the boundaries of my cell. I sat on the cell floor staring and inspecting each wall. Any graffiti? No. What were the textures? Nothing unusual. There was nothing to focus on or distract me from the situation. Even most of the other prisoners became silent. The feeling of powerlessness was overwhelming.

When it became time to sleep, despite having less than a foot to spare, I laid the pakama sideways in the middle of the cell. Lying this way kept my nose from the trough's toilet smell and avoided having my head next to the bars where the corridor light, although dimmed at night, flooded the front part of the cell. Trying to sleep with my head close to the bars with guards walking inches away would have been disturbing, but even more disconcerting were the new prisoners, often drunk and noisy, staggering to the bullpen close by my cell bars throughout the night.

The language barrier contributed to the solitude. Thai words have five different meanings depending on their tone, and this frustrated my efforts to speak fluently. Whenever I spoke Thai, because I am tone deaf, a listener had to discern my meaning primarily from the context of the conversation. In jail, there was no real context beyond trying to communicate basic needs to the guards.

Looking for anything to justify feeling optimistic, I discovered, toward the back of my cell, that if I bent a certain way, I could peer through a small crack between the floorboards and see grass a couple of feet below. That sight came to represent freedom: so close yet so far.

The only positive about being in jail alone is that you have time to reflect.

KILLING A DREAM

Sitting on the Thai jail floor, I wondered, *How did I get here?*

Arriving in Thailand almost four years ago, I intended to write a book on Thai business law. Shortly after that, however, I was invited to join the Kirkwood Bangkok law firm where I edited the first Thai Board of Investment book, *Doing Business in Thailand*. While there, I met Larry Andrews and Arthur Renander, who had just formed Gemex, an exploration and mining company. Andrews, a geologist, had bounced around South America and the Philippines and had come to Thailand to fulfill his dreams. Renander, a young, adventuresome and energetic New York lawyer, had taken leave from his promising legal and political career and joined Andrews to raise money for the business.

Impressed with my Thai business knowledge, they recruited me to run Spektron Laboratory, their mineral analysis subsidiary. According to Andrews, the laboratory would be successful because he had purchased a spectrograph machine, which he said was the only one of its kind in Thailand, thereby giving the company a monopoly position.

Over the subsequent months, my doubts about the company's direction grew as I watched Andrews spend most of his time entertaining several mid-level officials in the Department of Mineral Resources, whom he called his "Friends," rather than going into the field exploring. The Friends began going on the Gemex payroll in exchange for information and assistance in obtaining mining and exploration licenses. Based on the Friends' information, Andrews focused on acquiring lead and zinc mining licenses in Kanchanaburi Province and purchased a bulldozer and drill with loans from Chase Bank. When these exploration projects failed, he abruptly and illogically reversed course and switched to acquiring tin prospecting licenses offshore of Phuket, an entirely different exploration and mining activity for which Gemex had neither the equipment nor the staff, but where the Friends had licenses to sell.

Already twice divorced, Andrews had hired his Thai girlfriend, Chuansap, an attractive and ambitious young lady who helped create the "Friends" network and deliver their monthly payments. Like many foreign men, Andrews was proving susceptible to "going native," an occurrence which was usually accompanied by acquiring an exotic girlfriend who shaped their view of the Thai world. Having experienced this many times before, I recognized Chuansap's judgment was supplanting that of Andrews'.

None of the exploration licenses panned out and the company, having spent almost $1 million up to this point, had nothing to show for it. It was clear that most of the company's money was being used to support the lifestyles of Andrews, Chuansap, the Friends and, in turn, their friends who were the license owners.

The tipping point came when one of my Royal Bangkok Sports Club rugby teammates told me his inspection company also had a spectrograph machine. I visited his office, inspected the machine and found that it was the same model. When I reported this to Andrews, he smugly insisted, "Impossible. My Friends assured me that there is no other such machine in Thailand."

Even after I took both Renander and the company's only other American geologist to see the machine and both verified that it was identical, Andrews remained adamant and said we were all wrong. It was Andrew's flat-out denial of what was an unquestionable fact that erased any last remnant of his credibility and raised doubts about his mental stability.

Renander and I decided to replace Andrews at this point and Renander returned to the US to report our decision to the investors.

Becoming A Target

Aware of Renander's purpose, Andrews knew his survival depended on dividing Renander and me. Needing Renander's access to the investors and seeing my Thai experience as the principal threat to his control, Andrews targeted me. His first step was to fire me for insubordination and for 'being unacceptable' to the Friends. When Renander refused his cabled request for support in firing me, Andrews knew he had to take more drastic steps to discredit me.

Andrews enlisted Pradian, the Police Prosecuting General (equivalent to a Senior District Attorney) who had been leasing one of his houses to Andrews. With his income also in jeopardy, Pradian agreed to help Andrews and together they devised a plan to disgrace me publicly, thinking that would force me to leave Thailand.

A few days later, Chuansap took the office maid to the police station to file a report saying that I had sexually molested her. The police took no action, but someone tipped a newspaper to the allegation and they printed it. The next morning, being unaware of the report, I was shocked to read the accusation in the paper.

Renander immediately returned to Thailand and began investigating the charge. During his conversation with the maid, she disclosed the scheme. With the Andrews' dispute increasing in viciousness, Renander abandoned any effort to negotiate a reasonable termination with Andrews and immediately called for a Directors meeting to fire Andrews.

An angry and bitter Andrews and his group fought back. They orchestrated a plan to stop the Directors meeting by preventing a quorum. They paid the police to act on the molesting report and arrest me immediately before the start of the meeting.

Preecha, our Thai lawyer, who was present at the meeting, accompanied me to the police station where I was released after posting a $600 bond. Andrews' reprieve was brief because we rescheduled the interrupted meeting for the following day and fired Andrews. Knowing he could no longer postpone his termination, Andrews disappeared the previous night taking the company car, the company's share book and other property.

Andrews, with his resources dwindling, launched a wrongful termination lawsuit and the company counter-sued for the return of the company assets. After several months the cases were dismissed.

Pradian, however, as a matter of saving face, continued to pursue the molesting charge and despite the maid recanting her testimony, appealed the various verdicts dismissing the case. At one point, one judge suggested that if I just gave the maid $30, he would immediately stop all the appeals. I rejected the idea, explaining that such a deal might imply guilt which could hurt my future reputation. I ended up spending many times that amount before the Thai Supreme Court decision in my favor. As a matter of principle, I did successfully sue Andrews for defamation.

DOING RIGHT IS NOT WITHOUT RISKS

Gemex's investors had voted to liquidate the company assets so in between court appearances Renander and I had to wrap up the company's affairs. And the bank wanted the equipment loans repaid. Because of the hostilities, we took extra precautions, careful to ensure that the company's liquidation and equipment sales were transparent and that we followed all the proper legal procedures.

We hired a prominent accounting firm to audit the company's books and provide an independent third-party valuation of the equipment. We then sold the assets at those prices and paid the proceeds to the bank. The accounting firm conducted another audit following the sale showing the clean balance sheet with the loans paid and then we closed the company.

Little did we realize that Andrews would use that very transparency and detailed documentation to frame both

Renander and me.

That is why I was now in jail.

Andrews acquired copies of the audits, gave them to a police officer telling him that the audited statements proved that the equipment was in the company's possession at one point and was not there one month later, and that there was no money in the account. These audits, he claimed, were proof that Renander and I sold the assets and kept the money. Pocketing a $20 bribe, the police officer either did not understand or overlooked the fact that the money was used to pay off the loan, and so set out to arrest us. He assumed there was little risk to himself since Andrews told him that I would leave Thailand as a result of the arrest.

Trying to explain these transactions, describing what documents were available and their location over the static of the jail's visiting session chaos, was proving frustrating. Renander was unable to help since he would have been arrested as well on his arrival from the US.

I needed to get out of jail to fight this case.

THE PRICE OF FREEDOM

Obtaining bail was the next obstacle. Under Thai law, a person suspected of a crime can be kept in jail for up to 90 days for investigation before the police have to file formal charges. A person held on this basis, however, is brought to court every three or four days for a judge to determine if bail is appropriate and, if so, the amount. At this hearing, the police prosecutor either files formal charges or reports that the case is still under investigation. If the latter, he will make bail recommendations to the judge.

On the third day, I made my first trip to the court which was about an hour's drive through the Bangkok traffic. I was handcuffed, led to a pickup truck with a canvas top along with a couple of other prisoners, and locked to a railing. I could see all around as we drove and, despite the handcuffs, this was a welcome change from the monotony of the cell walls.

And sitting in the courtroom, I was finally able to have my first private conversations with Puttra and Preecha. Those strategy discussions stopped when the judge entered the courtroom followed by a prosecutor assigned by Pradian.

Per the prosecutor's request, the judge fixed the bail at the unusually high amount of $50,000, the estimated value of the equipment allegedly stolen. My hopes dropped when I heard the bail amount, the equivalent of $300,000 today.

But I don't need cash, just a bail bondsman, right?

Prior to the hearing, Puttra had arranged for a bail bondsman to post bond of a reasonable amount. With the bail set well beyond our bail bondsman's capacity, we would need a pledge of Thai real estate to back up the bail bond. Finding a Thai landowner who would be willing to risk a sizable portion of his real estate in a lawsuit with a complicated fact pattern and provide him with an assurance that I was not going to flee the country was going to be very difficult. We also had to find bail bondsman who would not be intimidated by Pradian.

Puttra finally found both, a landowner and bail bondsman who agreed to arrange the bond if I would escrow $50,000 cash as a guarantee that I would not forfeit bail.

I was now back to worrying about where I get the cash!

Neither my wife nor I have that kind of money.

My mother, who had just arrived in Bangkok and was not even aware that I was in jail, did not have much money and will not be able to do anything. Perhaps my brother, Marty, a law student, might be able to arrange a loan against my mother's house, even though she couldn't sign any papers.

And so I went back to jail.

MONEY CHALLENGE

The obstacles to raising this amount of money seemed insurmountable. The amount of money, the number of people involved, the faith they are going to need in this unusual situation, the time available, and the communication issues, may make getting this money impossible.

I have no idea what my wife's parents can do. I hope they can understand the situation.

Who are the other possible sources of money?

Who could contact them and what could they say?

While sitting on the cell floor, I listed as many of the problems that I could.

A significant communication problem is that there are only 12 telephone lines between Thailand and the United States. To call overseas, my wife would have to drive across Bangkok late at night to the Central Post Office and get in line to call the US. This meant she could only make a few calls a night.

How can she make sure that who she is calling will be available to answer at that time?

Answer: Perhaps cable in advance?

Can she describe the situation and answer any questions, especially since the events keep changing from one day to the next? I have only a couple of brief chances a day during the visiting hour bedlam to prepare her and others for the questions that I expect will be raised.

Answer: Scribble notes to pass to her.

At what point does she wear down?

Answer: Reduce her stress by remaining calm.

How will they get their money back?

Answer: They will get their money back if I am either released or go to jail.

As everyone was frantically arranging for the funds, I kept being carted back and forth to the court every couple of days to report on the bail struggle.

Remaining optimistic was hard. Surely tomorrow everything will get straightened out, I thought, but as the days passed, the word "tomorrow" was replaced by the words "soon" and "maybe."

Have Andrews and Pradian succeeded this time?

Are these barriers too much to overcome?

I had no idea of how, or when, all of this would end.

THE TIDE TURNS

But little by little, as everyone began to understand the facts, we started making progress. Things went from one step forward and two backward to one step forward and one step backward, and finally, two steps forward and one step backward. It was becoming clear to all parties that the arrest was fraudulent. There was no theft and I was not leaving Thailand.

One incident symbolized the shift. While playing rugby, I got to know Chamrat, a club director, who was also the third-highest ranking police officer in Thailand, outranking Pradian. In a nice gesture, he took time out of his busy schedule to come and inquire as to my wellbeing. He made the interesting comment that if I had murdered somebody, he could've gotten me released on a much lower bail, but since a judge set the bail, he could not lower the amount. The significance of his appearance, however, was not lost on the station's police officers and my treatment seemed to improve.

Family and friends mobilized to bring me food and drink at every visiting session. As much as I enjoyed Thai food, the jail food of a bowl of soup with some meat and a bowl of rice was generally unappetizing. Fortunately, there were no apparent restrictions on what food visitors could give to a prisoner. I did sleep well one night when some rugby teammates brought me vodka tonics in transparent plastic bags with the guards none the wiser.

FREEDOM

Finally, with Herculean efforts and contributions from many sources, $50,000 was deposited in a US bank and with the matching guarantee through a Thai bank, our new bail bondsman arranged the land guarantee.

On the 16th day, we went to court and presented the bond

evidence which was accepted by the judge. Within twenty minutes of this ruling, our bail bondsman got a spiteful call from Pradian's office saying that they would oppose his providing bail ever again.

I rode back to the police station in the same pickup truck, but this time without handcuffs.

At the station, a policeman returned my possessions without many words or much ceremony. I would like to think that perhaps the police were embarrassed by this whole affair, but I knew, like Pradian, it was important that they save face by continuing the charade.

Knowing that the case was not over until the 90-day investigation period passed tempered my sense of relief. It was unlikely that a formal charge would ever be filed since there was no theft. But I did not want to underestimate Andrews' determination and Pradian's manipulation of the legal system.

But for now, I walked out the station door, into the midday sun, a free man. I got in my car for the brief trip to my house which, for weeks, had seemed miles away.

AFTERWARD

While the Gemex litigation played out, I resumed my interest in a significant zinc deposit along the Burmese border in Northwest Thailand. As the Thai Communist insurgents were withdrawing from the area, I was able to visit the deposit site and collect the critical geological information. When the Thai government tendered the licenses covering the deposits later that year, we were prepared and won the bid.

We put together a partnership with three of Australia's largest companies: Electrolytic Zinc Australasian, BHP, and Anglo-American Australia...and when they withdrew, we partnered with New Jersey Zinc to start mining operations and design a zinc refinery. For the next several years, our company, Thai Zinc, became the flagship project for foreign investment in Thailand.

Personally, I was elected president of the American Chamber of Commerce in Thailand and then elected Chairman of the Asia Pacific Council of American Chambers of Commerce. As the US and China began its rapprochement, I led the first delegation of American businessmen that had been invited to the China Trade Fair in 1977. A year later, at the request of the US government, I hosted a formal luncheon for Vice President Walter Mondale and the regional US ambassadors at the opening of the US Embassy in Guangzhou, China in 1979.

Toasting US-China friendship with Maotais, the national drink of China, in a formal ceremonial dining room was a long distance from drinking a vodka tonic alone on a Thai jail floor!

For over 47 years Arthur Renander and I have continued to help each other through many trials and tribulations.

Andrews was never heard from again.

A. REBECCA WAGNER

Author's Note: This piece is an excerpt from *Saving Ember*, a novel in the making. It tells the story of Ember Fisher, a mentally ill teenager battling severe schizophrenia. Plagued by visions of ghoulish, deformed monsters and tormented by the cruel and mocking voices of her invisible masters, Lilith and M'kesh, fifteen year old Ember is convinced she is on the verge of being consumed by an army of ravenous insects hiding inside her.

On the edge of a complete and devastating breakdown, Ember's only refuge from the madness eclipsing her world is a pack of wolves and the Alaskan wilderness. In these pages, she flees to the tundra during a particularly horrific episode, in search of her pack for comfort and protection from the horrors of a disease she doesn't yet understand.

I have personally struggled with mental illness for the last twenty years and am all too familiar with the dark, ugly ways it can warp a person's mind, so I feel Ember's story is an important one to be told. This is an issue that should be dragged into the light and discussed openly, without stigma, so those who are struggling can know that they are not alone and have a fair chance at a life full of light and love. None of us should be forced to suffer in silence.

For Sarah and Julie, my childhood friends who pulled me through in the very beginning, memories of Grove Street, love potion, bonfires and pet shops still occupy my fondest remembrance of us. I also want to shout from the rooftops my immense gratitude for Andi and Dijana, who both stepped into my life when I was just a lonely, troubled teenager who desperately needed someone in her corner. I still think of you both when I drive off to "get lost" and stand on the summit of Mount Agamenticus. To everyone at Coastal, Brian, Pam, Marci, Tami, Joelle, Gordon, Paul F, Paul W and all my former classmates, all I have left to say is thank you. Lastly, my deepest and greatest love goes to James and Victor, without whom I would be nothing: you are my everything, my entire world, my heart and soul, and you both fill each of my days with love and joy I never imagined could be mine. I will always love you biggest.

Saving Ember

BY THE TIME THE GIRLS GOT BACK TO TOWN, the snow was falling hard, accumulating heavily on the streets and sidewalks.

Ember shivered violently, not from the biting January cold, but from the insects, which she felt stirring inside her.

Fear, she'd discovered the night her mother had nearly caught her hurting herself, made them angry.

The watchers had followed them into the woods, a place that used to be hers. A sacred place. They haunted her everywhere she went, but at least she'd had the woods. Now she wasn't safe anywhere. She was terrified and the insects sensed it.

They reached Raven's house first and parted ways, Ember barely uttering a word as she shuffled away in the direction of home. The stop there was brief, dropping her poles and shoes in the mudroom and then up to her bedroom, grabbing her most treasured and vital possessions, her pocketknife and flashlight.

She buried the pocketknife deep in her parka pocket and slipped out the back door before her parents had a chance to notice her. She couldn't stay there. Even though the watchers were out there somewhere, she had to get out. She couldn't risk bringing the insects to life.

Snow blasted her in the face as she burst out the back door. It barely fazed her as she bounded down the steps, up the driveway and into the street.

Gotta get away, gotta get away, she chanted in her mind as she sprinted towards the square. The freezing temperature wrestled against the heavy fabric of her parka, desperate to lay its frost bitten chill against the delicate warmth of her flesh. But she feared the insects dwelling within her were far more powerful than even the brutal force of an arctic winter and she didn't dare tempt them. They could consume her from the inside out. Movement, so far, was the only thing that kept them satiated.

Walking faster, Ember let out an exasperated and flustered yelp, similar to the sounds the pups made when they were younger and being reprimanded by the adults. She squinted through the thick snowfall and thrust her gloved hands into her pockets, her right hand squeezing the pocketknife hard. She had to get to the tundra, find a safe place, and try to rid herself of the insects. Miniscule time bombs squirming around inside her: they were going to kill her if she didn't get them out.

As she hurried through the square and passed by Richdales, she spied something move out of the corner of her eye. She froze, daring to look behind her.

It was quicker than lightening, gone in the bat of an eye, but she saw it, ducking behind the corner of the squat, brick building like it wanted to be noticed at the very last minute.

The burning, fiery sockets of its empty skull stood out like a sore thumb against the white blankness of the frozen landscape. Ignited by the darkening evening sky, even its handless arms, somehow gripping the brick, seemed to glow in the descending gloom, silently challenging her to approach it.

Ember, however, was nowhere near that brave. "Go away!

You have no right to keep following me!" She screamed and flipped it the bird, sensing it roar in anger and retreat into the shadows for now.

She raced fast to the tundra, feeling it behind her the rest of the way.

'Run girl, run!' Lilith and M'kesh taunted in time to her frantic pace. 'Run like a fool! You can't escape them!'

At last she made it to the snow covered plain, their voices egging her on through the storm. The flakes fell faster than she could blink, collecting in her eyelashes and stinging her eyes.

Too frightened to slow down, she snapped her head around to see if she'd lost the watchers, subsequently losing her footing and falling face first into the deep snow.

She rolled over, sputtering and wiping snow from her eyes. It was so cold she was surprised by the fact that it was already melting on her face. Then it she realized it wasn't snow that was wetting her cheeks. They were tears. She hadn't even noticed she was crying.

She lay still for as long as she could stand it, letting the sobs go and welcoming the barrage of snowflakes as they engulfed her like an icy blanket. She hoped it might hide her from the watchers. But she knew it wouldn't.

'Weakling,' Lilith growled in disgust.

'Pitiful,' M'kesh said.

Sniffling, Ember sat up and struggled to her feet. "Shut up. Both of you just shut up," she whispered through gritted, chattering teeth.

'Watch your mouth, little girl,' M'kesh roared back. 'Our friends are coming for you!'

She was so cold she could barely move, but somehow she staggered to her feet. She had to keep going. She was too still for too long. The insects were stirring.

She tried to run but the snow was so high she stumbled every few steps. Cursing herself for leaving her snowshoes behind, she trudged onward, the sound of crunching snow in the background getting closer. A few clumsy feet later, the strength drained from her body, she sensed the watchers closing in and the insects getting hungry; Ember realized she was out of options. She needed her wolf pack.

She collapsed in the snow, tossed back her head and howled. Her cry seemed to echo clear across the tundra, slicing through the falling flakes and boomeranging off the white-washed peaks of the Alaska Range.

She howled again and again, stretching out the notes and listening to her voice sweep across the top of the snow. The freezing air stung her throat, but she couldn't stop. She needed the wolves to find her.

Despite her exhaustion, she picked herself up and pushed on through the drifts, howling and searching, ripping off her gloves and unzipping her parka. The icy winds bum rushed her, whipping through the thick sweater underneath as if she were naked.

She had to do something. She still wasn't moving fast enough. Mired in the snow banks, each step agonizingly slow, Ember sensed their hunger about to erupt. She stopped, reached under her sweater and raked her fingernails across her skin, imagining scooping out the creatures and dumping them into the snow. Since she didn't know what they actually looked like, she imagined handfuls of spiders and beetles, twisting and wriggling in her palms, angrily fighting their freezing demise outside of her.

She scratched herself raw, barely noticing as she began to tremble and shake in the subzero temperature. The tiny invaders burrowed in her gut seemed satisfied for the moment, but she knew better. The hunger was only getting stronger. They had to come out.

Starting to feel the cold numbing her hands and racking her body, she thrust her hands into her pockets, curling her freezing fingers around the pocketknife. They had to come out.

Something moaned in the smothering winter darkness beyond. Ember gripped the knife in her pocket, briefly thinking that she could use it as a weapon. *Idiot,* her thoughts berated her. *Get that close and you're dead. Its got you. What the hell are you thinking?*

Something heavy dragged itself through the snow, blazing red holes piercing the blackness. The wind gusted and blew its sickening stench into her face, violently turning her stomach. Not knowing what else to do, she howled again, hoping it would drive away the corpse-like thing tracking her. Where were the wolves?

She pulled the flashlight from her other pocket, shining it through the heavy snow fall, hoping to catch the glimmer of approaching wolf eyes. Then, like a lightbulb filling the darkest corners of her mind with light, she remembered.

"Ember's Reach!" It was a risky climb after dark, but she had no choice. It was the only place left for her.

"Ember's Reach!" She shouted again, almost laughing. "How could I forget? Ember's Reach is mine. All mine!"

So she ran, her temporary high granting her a momentary burst of speed and dexterity over the building drifts. Her jacket still hung open, flapping in the wind, her gloves now gone and claimed by the snow, but she continued to laugh.

At the base of the foothill that ascended to the Reach, Ember barely hesitated. Upward and onward she plowed, following the yellow beam of light up the perilous incline.

With slipping boots and frost-bitten hands that were practically frozen to the flashlight, she was eventually guided to exactly where she needed to be: Ember's Reach.

"Yes!" She cried, not sure how to handle the overwhelming joy. She hardly recalled how it felt these days and was paralyzed in the moment. Her mind drew a blank, and as she stood there rather stupidly in the whiteout, all she could do was laugh some more.

The somewhat crazy sounding laughter bubbled from her lips as she finally climbed up and onto the ridge, stumbled past the barren trees and fell to her knees dangerously close to the edge.

Ember buried her face in her frozen hands, her fingers so cold they actually stung her cheeks. She hardly noticed however, just laughed louder and louder. She felt like she couldn't stop.

Even as the refreshing intermission faded and misery reclaimed her, as the insects clustered beneath her skin and their hunger resurfaced, she laughed.

Even as icy tears trickled from her eyes and slid down her cheeks, she continued to laugh. She felt deranged. Insane.

Stop it! Her mind screamed. *Just stop it! What is wrong with you?*

'Get it now?' M'kesh's voice cut through her laughter. 'We're in control. You will do exactly as you're told. You answer to us.'

Ember grunted and collapsed. She felt even more powerless than when they'd blasted those terrible images of Raven's murder into her brain, leaving her so paralyzed that at first she wasn't sure if she'd actually attacked her best friend.

She pushed her face into the snow, sucking in mouthfuls, choking out the laughter. With a tremendous burst of mental strength, she finally forced her vocal cords to shift gears and as she pulled herself back onto her knees, she turned her face to the snowy sky and resumed howling, praying the wolves would find her.

Finally, another howl cut through the night. It was Talon, his wild call nearly as deep now as his father's, the great Denali.

Wilder and Sakari called out next, sounding much closer. Her heart raced at their reply. She called back to the two wolves, indicating where she was.

They played a vocal game of tag, their voices melding together like a beautiful, wild symphony. Her howl was so polished that someone listening could have easily assumed she was one of the wolves.

Ember turned toward the tree line behind her. They were close. Then, shapes moving in the snow. Gleaming yellow eyes.

She called out weakly, "I'm here!"

There was a gruff bark and two large grey wolves burst forth from the snow, tongues rolling and tails wagging.

She opened her arms and let the wolves crash into her,

knocking her back down. They licked her face and nuzzled her body, yelping with pleasure.

"Oh, Sakari, Wilder," she purred. "Thank you. Thank you. I need you so much right now. I need you to protect me. There are bad things after me."

Phantom's eyes appeared next, two hovering yellow orbs in the dark, his white body virtually invisible in the raging snowfall. The three remaining pups, Talon, Jewel and Sapphire appeared behind him and greeted her in a frenzy, bombarding her with their warm, comforting bodies.

"Hey pups!" She cried, tears of joy wetting her saliva-caked cheeks. His tail whipping in elation, alpha pup Talon stood over her, head cocked, eyes questioning.

Ember reached up and stroked his neck, smiling. "It's okay, Talon. Just another bad day. I'll be okay as long as I'm with you."

He yipped and circled around her, nudging her with his nose. He finally lay down beside her and the other pups did the same, forming a circle around the shivering girl. She was so scared and fatigued, she'd hardly noticed her body lapsing into uncontrollable shaking.

She did notice the commanding and impressive figures of Denali and Cassiopeia standing over her. She smiled up at the alphas, who gazed upon her with wolfish grins and flicking tails.

"Hey, mom. Hey, dad," she whispered. The words stung her throat, but the sight of the two wolves filled her heart with bliss. "I was hoping you'd come. I'm so grateful you found me up here."

Cassiopeia lowered her head and ran her rough, warm tongue across Ember's face and rubbed her cheeks with her muzzle, a gesture that signified true comradery. In return, she rubbed the side of the she-wolf's head, her fingers swimming through her velvety soft pelt.

"I love you," she whispered again. "You're such a gorgeous momma."

Denali trotted up to her and thrust his cold, wet nose against hers. Then he opened his jaws and gently clamped his teeth around her chin, mouthing her lower jaw as a sign of ultimate wolf love and respect.

She giggled as he broke it off and she offered her throat, showing the hulking black wolf the greatest sign of respect a human could offer.

Denali went for it, but never to hurt her. His tongue rolled over her like the balmiest summer breeze, comforting her like a beloved childhood blanket. She wrapped her arms around his muscular neck and sighed contently, wishing she could bottle this fleeting wisp of happiness and stash it in her heart forever.

The furry bodies gathered around her had warmed her considerably and for the moment, she felt safe. That was until she happened to glance across the tundra and noticed them.

There were dozens, she had never seen so many at once. Moving in small groups scattered across the blustery land below, hordes of watchers had somehow discovered her hideaway. Now an entire army of the ghastly things were coming for her.

Ember screamed and scrambled backwards, far from the edge of the reach. This startled the wolves and they all jumped to their feet, rushing to her side. An agitated Sapphire nosed Ember's shoulder and licked her cheek, whining deep in her throat.

"I'm sorry, girl," she apologized, patting the top of her head. "But they're...they're coming. They must have followed me. I was so sure I lost them!"

Denali and Wilder stood close to the edge, looking down over the tundra. Their watchful eyes swept the snow scape, probably spurred by Ember's panic.

But something wasn't right. Their tails weren't raised in alarm and they both appeared calm.

She didn't understand. She'd seen the adults raise the alarm before, when they'd scented strange wolves in their territory or other wolves were spotted sniffing around the den the previous summer when the pups were young. The results were always exposed jaws and snarling teeth, pancaked ears and hacklecrested backs.

Why weren't they reacting now, why were they not alerting the rest of the pack of the impending danger?

Maybe the watchers weren't a threat to the wolves and they had no reason to fear them. It made sense, seeing as they'd vanished both times when Raven and her mom had appeared.

The realization that they were only out for her sent her spirits crashing to the ground. That meant she was in this battle alone and no one could help, possibly not even the wolves.

Ember knew that on her own she would never make it.

'That's the idea. They work for us, you know.' M'kesh's voice called from a distance. 'We control their every move, just as we do yours. When they do come for you, it will be on our orders. And they will come for you.'

The wolves weren't reacting to M'kesh, either. They seemed distressed, but she guessed that was because of her reaction.

She crawled back towards the ledge and dared to peek down. She screamed again and scuttled backwards. Even in the midst of such severe conditions, they were unmistakable amongst the stark white landscape. They had multiplied so fast she couldn't even count them. Every inch of the tundra was covered with dragging, rotting bodies. There had to be hundreds, shuffling steadily across the tundra in a zombie like trance.

It was a parade out of her worst nightmare, the floodgates of hell opening and sending all of its most insidious inhabitants on a mission to drag her back to their fiery prison.

The sickening crimson beams shooting from their eyeless sockets seemed to lead the march. They had never appeared to her with actual eyes, but the vacant, shining holes were far worse.

She was trapped. There was no way she could safely flee through the woods behind her in this weather. The only way home was across the tundra. Through THEM.

"Please, make them go away," she begged, cowering feebly in the snow. "I'll do anything. Just don't let them hurt me."

Lilith replied, sounding closer than M'kesh. 'Now, why

would I do that? What a tragic waste of such efficient killing machines. They are capable of things your fragile little mind can't even comprehend.'

"Please, call them off," she sobbed, heaving tearfully into the snow. "I don't want to die up here. I can't get down. Lilith. M'kesh. Please!"

She was freaking out and now so were the wolves. They circled her, howling and yipping. Their ears and tails were raised for her as they nudged and pawed at her body.

Talon shoved his black muzzle against Ember's face, whimpering and licking her salty tears as they fell.

"I'm sorry," she whispered to the frantic animal. "I know you don't understand. There are horrible things out there. And they won't stop. They'll never stop."

But she knew she couldn't stay on Ember's Reach all night. Not without her parents freaking out and probably grounding her. She could never stay in her house that long, especially now with the watchers ready to rip her to shreds.

And it was far too cold to be anywhere outside. Even surrounded by wolves, she would never survive the night.

That left only one choice. She had to run for it. Even if it meant colliding with the mob head on. It was the only way home.

"Okay, guys," she told the wolves. "I really don't want to do this. They're going to tear me apart. But I have no other way."

She took a deep breath and peered over the edge one last time. She didn't scream this time, just blinked and rubbed her eyes.

They were gone. Every last one of them. Just as suddenly as they'd appeared, they had vanished back into nowhere.

"H-how?" She sputtered, desperately wiping snow from her eyes. "They were just there! That's impossible!" She turned to the wolves, more frightened tears rolling down her cheeks.

The pack gathered by the edge with her. Sandwiched between their strong, protective bodies, Ember sobbed speechlessly as they howled. They seemed to howl for her, as if warning the watchers to never return.

Lilith and M'kesh cackled from somewhere. 'You'll never see it coming,' they laughed. 'Don't you worry your pretty little head about a way home. Your new home will be with us. Your pathetic pets can't save you.'

"I will!" She yelled out. "I will see it coming! I'll be ready for anything! In her heart, Ember knew that wasn't true. She was already tired and weak. How could she fight such an impossible army?

"And leave my wolves alone, both of you," she added daringly, trying her hardest to sound bold. What actually came out sounded puny and small. "They've done nothing to you."

Lilith and M'kesh simply laughed. They continuously goaded her as she crawled off Ember's Reach, slipping and staggering down the hillside.

The wolves followed every step of the way, Denali in front, leading her down like one of the pack. She tried to focus on his furry black tail, waving in the wind like a helping hand pointing the safest way out. But Lilith and M'kesh screamed at her all the way down.

Back on the flat tundra, the wolves stayed with her the whole way across. Tonight they came even closer to town. All eight wolves seemed skittish, but they followed at her side nonetheless.

Her heart hammering against her ribs, she stared into the darkness around her, petrified, scanning the landscape for those gleaming red sockets. Ember moved as fast as she could, tripping through the drifts.

At the edge of town, parting with the wolves was hard, but she didn't dare linger. The watchers could reappear at any second.

"I have to go," she whispered nervously. "I know they'll be back. They're always waiting. Be careful out here. I'll be back as soon as I can."

Talon, Sapphire and Jewel reared up on their hind legs, all trying to rest their paws on Ember's shoulders at once. They pressed their muzzles into her neck, all three tongues caressing her chin and cheeks.

"I love you, too," she assured them quietly, running her hands down their flanks. "All of you. I would be lost without you. Keep a listen out for me."

The wolves howled a long, sad note as she returned to Frost Point. Somewhere in between those parting cries was the crazed bellowing of Lilith and M'kesh, rising up between the screaming winter winds and blowing directly into her brain.

She charged through the whiteout, the watchers returning and trailing her the whole way. They stayed hidden this time but nothing could block that smell or drown out those sounds.

Her parents immediately noticed how upset she was, probably by the way she burst into the house, ripped off her boots, threw them against the wall and ran upstairs without saying a word, not even bothering to take her coat off.

"You missed dessert!" Oliver cried as she whipped through the living room, building some type of castle out of Lego bricks. "Mommy made strawberry jello!"

How she wished strawberry jello could still solve all her problems. Jelly jumped up from her velvet dog bed by the hearth and hurtled over to greet her in a fuzzy blur, but Ember only shooed her away and rushed the rest of the way up to her room. If they weren't intimidated by an entire pack of wild wolves, then there wasn't a thing her goofy Akita could do to defend her against the watchers.

Ember slammed her door shut and slipped her hand into her pocket, pulling out the pocketknife. She had to do this while the hunger was mild.

Switching on the lamp on her desk, she tore off her parka and hurled it across the room, landing on the edge of her bed.

'Ready?' Lilith breathed in her ear. 'Are you ready to give those little bastards what's coming to them?'

Ember whimpered and nodded. She was ready. Just then someone knocked and the doorknob turned. Ember shoved the pocketknife under her pillow just as her mom, Lynn, stepped inside.

Lilith screamed in protest. Where was it coming from? The closet? Under the bed? Outside the window? She could never tell.

Lynn didn't react. Instead, she sat down on the bed beside her daughter. "Honey, are you alright? We never talk anymore and I feel like something is wrong."

"Nope, nothing at all. Absolutely nothing," she muttered, trying not to squirm. "Not a thing."

"There never used to be any secrets between us, remember? Nothing's changed, Ember. I'm still your mom and I love you."

Everything's changed, Ember wanted to scream in her face. *I feel like I've been shredded by a hundred sharks and there are random pieces of me everywhere! My wholeness is gone. I don't think I'll ever be right again.* But she didn't, just kind of grunted, nodded and stared anxiously at her pillow. If her mom really felt that way, she would already know what was wrong.

"I just want you to be honest with me," Lynn pleaded, stroking her daughter's hair. "Please don't be afraid to come to me. I just want to know you're ok."

I'm tired," Ember said, wringing her hands in her lap. "Can I go to bed now? I'm really tired. I mean it."

"Okay. I'm sorry." She still didn't sound convinced. Before she got up to leave, she held Ember's twitching hands and said, "Just talk to me, okay? I'm here for you. Promise me that."

"Okay," she mumbled, the hunger rising to the surface of her flesh like plumes of smoke from a fiery disaster that was breaking out inside her. Her fear breathed new life into them. They had to come out.

Her mom left, closing the door behind her. Finally, she was alone. Well, not really alone.

M'kesh spoke, his voice ripe with glee. 'Better hurry. They're ravenous little things. They'll pick you apart till there's nothing left.'

"No!" She cried and pulled her pocketknife out from under the pillow. Suddenly the urge to hide overwhelmed her. Her eyes darted around the tiny room, panicked and confused. Had they followed her inside?

'The light!' Lilith screeched so loud her voice cracked. 'Turn it off! Turn out the light!'

"Why?" Ember whimpered. "I...I don't want to." Those beaming scarlet holes. Empty. Sinister. Dead. She couldn't face that in the dark. Alone. "They'll get me in the dark."

'The dark will protect you,' Lilith hissed. 'We will see they stay away for now. But only in the dark. They can't find you in the dark.'

She hated the dark. But if she disobeyed, her masters would let them in. So she leaned over and switched the lamp off, plunging her into that gruesome darkness.

'Now then,' Lilith said, sighing contently. 'Where were we?'

Ember dove to the floor and crawled over to the window, dragging herself to the only light source in the room, the window at the end of her bed. Between the nearly full moon and the streetlight, a comforting streaming of light awaited her and for a second or two, she echoed Lilith's contentment in a sigh of her own.

Then the hunger flared and she stood up, pulling off her sweater so fast it got tangled around her face and she panicked, thinking they had somehow trapped her. She finally yanked it off and threw it across the room with a shriek to join her discarded parka. Her jeans came next and within minutes she had stripped down to nothing but her bra and panties. It was the only way to ensure she got them all out.

She dropped to the floor, shaking, hunched against the foot of her bed. She slid open the pocket knife, revealing a gleaming metallic blade. It was beautiful to her, the only thing that brought her peace, the one object she couldn't live without.

'Now there, Ember, our sweet little Ember,' M'kesh purred, his voice gentle, soothing. 'Are we ready? I think it's time to flush out those hideous parasites. They're going to devour you.'

'Do you feel them in there? Scrambling for nutrients, moving, crawling?' Lilith's voice was soft, almost sensual. The only time they weren't nasty was when she cut. 'They are about to feed.

What are we going to do about it?'

The light streamed over her, a silvery cascade of moonlight, spotlighting her grand attempt to free herself from the invasion. She held up the sharp blade, the star of the show, freckled with bits of dried blood, stark reminders of dark, desperate moments.

She brought it down swiftly, the serrated edge dragging across her skin. Her heart pounded and she breathed heavily as that dark red substance seeped from the torn skin of her forearm.

They could get out now.

'Good girl,' M'kesh said. 'But I'm afraid that's not enough. You're infested. You need to keep going. It's the only way, unless you want them to devour you?'

Ember whimpered no. Cloaked in the darkness of her room, shaking and crying in a shower of lonely gray light cast across her floor, she held the blade over her other arm.

She winced as the hunger flared.

ELIZABETH KILCOYNE

Author's Note: A Stone in My Pocket is a heroine's journey. It begins with an ordinary person looking for more meaning in her life. She needs to get away by herself, out of the routine of daily tasks, and do some inner searching. Life as she knows it is unacceptable. The Camino de Santiago has been calling pilgrims to experience this arduous journey since the 9th century. It promised to test and reward all who walk it. This is a true story.

A Stone in My Pocket

ON THE 28TH DAY OF MY JOURNEY on the Camino de Santiago, I was reviewing my life's burdens, one by one. My thirty year marriage had ended, my younger daughter was angry with me because I divorced her father, I was 62 years old and I had no idea where my life was going. I had been walking for three hundred and forty miles, and now was my chance to finally leave these burdens behind, but could I?

People have been walking the Camino since the 9th century, seeking cures from the apostle Saint James for illnesses such as tuberculosis, typhoid and influenza. The walk's purpose has evolved since then: from seeking cures to searching for the meaning of life. In 2011, over a hundred thousand people walked the Camino, and I was one of them.

El Camino de Santiago, The Way of Saint James, is a 500 mile pilgrimage located in northern Spain. It begins in St. Jean Pied-de-Port in the foothills of the Pyrenees on the French border and ends in Santiago de Compostela, almost to the Atlantic Ocean. People who walk this journey are referred to as pilgrims as they are on a mission to touch the tomb of Saint James to receive a sense of comfort. Saint James was the apostle beheaded in Jerusalem by King Herod, and as the story goes was buried by his disciples in what is now known as Santiago de Compostela. Pilgrims spend each night in albergues, similar to hostels after their long days.

PREPARATIONS

A few months before I left for the Camino, I read blogs to help with preparations. Walking twelve miles a day for thirty-eight days with everything I needed on my back seemed extreme. I was practically a senior citizen. Walking was my favorite pastime, but 500 miles? I had to do something. I was no stranger to the Camino. My older daughter and I spent five days walking it in 2006. After those blissful days we felt rejuvenated and peaceful all at once. My current life situation needed more of that.

I was a successful consultant and by all appearances happy with my new life. I put a new kitchen in the house; I went out to dinner with friends and spent time with my children. The truth is I was on autopilot. I was asleep. Filling my time with so many activities, I was seldom in touch with myself or my feelings. I kept saying, *just keep moving forward*. And that usually worked until I was alone. One Saturday afternoon I was refinishing my kitchen cabinets and started to panic because I didn't have plans for the weekend. I called my brother, "Hey, I know Dorothy's away. Do you want to come to Ipswich tonight for the river illumination celebration?"

He said, "Sorry honey, it's been a big day and I'm too tired to drive up there tonight."

I called at least four other people but had to leave messages. Then I called my daughter in Oregon just to talk to someone and said, "I can't call anyone else, they'll think I'm desperate at five o'clock on a Saturday afternoon."

She said, "Mom, your friends never think you're desperate." I didn't call anyone else.

Have you ever been so lonely, you could scream? Well, I did scream, many times. Where was I going? What was the purpose of my life? I was only 62. Life couldn't be over yet. I was scared that mine was. Something had to change.

So, I continued preparing my body for the Camino. According to one blog, maintaining your feet was key to a walker's success. This advice came from a twenty three year old: "Apply body glide entirely over feet and ankles before walking and again at lunch. Change socks at lunch. Wear light hiking boots in the morning and running shoes in the afternoon."

Growing up Catholic helps when you need to follow directions; I was faithful to this plan every day and as pilgrims all around me were nursing blisters, I never got one. Of course the downside was that a second pair of shoes in my pack meant leaving something behind. My shoulders could only handle ten pounds at the time. Could I get on with one set of clothes for walking and some yoga pants and top for after walking and sleeping? Some pilgrims had their packs transported from one albergue to the next. Would that make sense for me?

I wanted to walk by myself, feel the breeze, see the sunsets, meet other pilgrims and learn their stories. I needed alone time, but being a woman prevented me from feeling comfortable walking alone through the isolated areas of a country so far from home. I was afraid. Even the pepper spray I bought wasn't enough to make me comfortable walking alone. It didn't occur to me that having other people along would interfere with my experience.

A group email resulted in four people offering to walk with me for a week or two each: Lynn, a friend from choir would start with me; David, a retired friend from Ipswich would join me in Logroño; my cousin from Canada would arrive in Leon; and my older daughter, Meg, would finish with me. That would leave some days walking alone, which I didn't realize I would treasure.

The Beginning

"You may have a fresh start any moment you choose, for this thing called 'failure' is not the falling down, but the staying down."
- Mary Pickford

Lynn and I started the Camino de Santiago on September 5th, 2011. Our spirits were up and we were ready for adventure. The first mountain was over 3,000 feet and food was scarce. The guide book had identified cafes along the way, but some were closed or had limited hours after the high summer season. As we rested on a bridge, Lynn said, "Is that a vending machine over there?"

We rushed over to find that it only had Coke and beer! After that we were never without food again! By day three, we were dragging our feet under the weight of our packs. I had trained four days a week for three months, walking with my pack six to ten miles each time, but this was an arduous journey.

On a deserted riverbank outside of Pamplona we were taking a break when a hysterical woman and her daughter came by. The mother said, "Did you see that man in the red shirt?"

"Yes," we said.

"He was making inappropriate comments and eyes at my daughter," she said.

"Rest with us for a while."

Lynn and I had seen the man walk past. He was talking to himself and gesturing, but didn't seem like a threat, at least to us. Our new friends, Gabi and her daughter Laura, were from Germany, walking the Camino before Laura went off to college. We continued on our walk. We each carried a weapon of sorts: 2 knives, a pen, and pepper spray. We were prepared for trouble. The man in the red shirt was standing down by the river masturbating. A Camino lesson: you only need to worry about strangers on the Camino that don't carry a pack! After a while, we lost track of Gabi and Laura, which often happens on the Camino. People walk faster or slower or pause to meditate. I hoped that our paths would cross again.

There are churches in every town along the Camino with the evening rosary starting at 7:30 and a Pilgrim Mass at 8:00. The older ladies can be heard all over town chanting *Santa Maria*. Mary is the center of all the churches. Christ is there, but Santa Maria is the matriarch! Even though I no longer practiced Catholicism, mass was a memorable ritual of the journey.

FORGIVING

"Without forgiveness, there's no future."
- Desmond Tutu

We climbed Alto del Perdón, or Mt. Forgiveness, 1,000 feet to the summit. On the way up Mt. Forgiveness I thought about all the people I needed forgiveness from and prayed that I would receive it. On the way down, I thought about all the people that I should forgive and prayed that I would give it.

I needed forgiveness from my children for divorcing their father. My older daughter Meg seemed to be accepting. She recently told me she wondered why it took me so long. Her sister Anna was only 18 at the time and it hit her harder. I'm hoping time and love will help her. I also needed to forgive myself. I thought I had destroyed the family by being selfish and needing to fulfill my life. Learning to forgive can help us heal, and I needed healing in order to move forward. I was lonely and sad and was becoming a poor role model for my daughters. This was not the way life should be. Being asleep was easy. No introspection. No soul-searching. No deep feelings. But I needed more. I hoped that forgiving myself would be the first step.

The descent from Mt. Forgiveness was full of loose stones, making going down quite tricky. Lynn was suffering from the heat and terrain so we sang show tunes to keep our spirits up until her part of the journey ended.

There are three ways to travel the Camino: by foot, bike or horseback. So far I've seen many walkers, a couple of bikers, but no pilgrims on horseback. We did meet Pepe, a self-appointed Camino angel, who had done the Camino twice, the first time on a white horse, the second time on foot. Now he parked his truck full of coffee and water and berries and other treats along deserted parts of The Way for hungry pilgrims.

On the way to Villamayor de Monjardin I met a retired couple from Canada, Deann and René. They were singing, so of course I joined right in. We arrived at an albergue in the early afternoon and spent the rest of the day on a garden terrace off our room. All around us there were mountains, villages, farms and churches under a sunny sky. A Japanese couple who didn't speak English arrived when René and I were trying to remember the words to the song *The Times They are a Changin'*. The man pulled out an mp3 player and played the song. We invited them to sit with us.

The hosts of the albergue were volunteers from a Dutch ecumenical group. They had a short prayer time in the evening, which some folks found a bit pushy, but five days in, I was open to the experiences the Camino was offering. I didn't know where my life was going and that's why I was there. I thought I would be thinking more about my life, but the truth is I was focused on getting to the next albergue to rest my feet and back. As I walked, the encumbrances of life did drift away. No lists. No work projects. No commitments. Just walking in the beauty of this romantic country. Back in the room, I dragged my mattress out onto the terrace and slept under the stars. Sleep came easily.

Missing Out

We left the next morning in the dark and arrived in Torres de Rio by early afternoon. It was the type of terrain I dreamed the Camino would be - dirt path through open farmland and vineyards. I didn't have many regrets on the Camino, but one was being afraid to walk alone. My need for security made me miss the "running of the bulls" that day in Los Arcos. Runners in white shirts and pants with red sashes gathered; women dressed in festive outfits carried tall replicas of saints, while others installed the gates along the street that protected the spectators and businesses. You could feel the excitement in the air. I tried to talk Deann and René into staying, but they wanted to move along before the heat of the day. Under other circumstances I would have agreed to move on, but this was the running of the bulls and I wanted to stay; regrettably, we trekked on. I was so disappointed and angry with myself. I didn't just miss the bulls, I missed the opportunity to make memories with others, hear their stories and maybe free myself up a bit.

I could feel every mile. The open fields continued; most of the harvesting was complete, leaving behind wispy fields of hay. Deann and René had been very generous to me. They were going to take a rest day. I hated to say goodbye, but it felt good to give them back to each other and to their Camino.

Onward

On day seven David arrived from Ipswich and we stayed in the Inglesia de Santiago church house, an albergue that relied on donations and we slept on floor mats. Most albergues charged between 6 and 10 euros, or $7.50 and $12, which made the trip more affordable. Later that evening I noticed I'd lost my Camino passport at the last stop on the way into Logroño. The passport is stamped at albergues and churches along The Way as proof that one walked the Camino. I thought about going back for the passport, but since the Camino is about moving forward, I got a new passport and trekked on.

We stopped in Navarrette where there is a 16th century Church of the Assumption with a gold leaf alter that covered the entire front wall of the church. Mary, as always, was center stage. As luck would have it, we ran into Gabi and Laura. We embraced like sisters! The Camino is a journey where pilgrims move forward at their own pace and reunions are hoped for but not always guaranteed.

We gathered around a dinner of ensalada, potatoes, bacon, and wine cooked by a young German man. He was financing his way along the Camino by making dinner for pilgrims. That evening we received a pilgrim blessing in the gold church. The Mass was in Spanish and Latin. I remembered a little Spanish from college and Latin from Catholic school, but it didn't matter, for the spirit of the message was clear: safe journey. When the priest gave the Pilgrim Blessing, he asked us for our native languages, and blessed us in each one. There were at least ten languages!

ROUTINE STUFF

Bars are open all day on the Camino, serving breakfast in the morning and then alcohol and food the rest of the day. I picked up the menu and it was the same as the last bar. I had a Spanish omelet and Nestea every day.

Bathrooms are a challenge on the Camino. We peed in the bar restrooms, behind gigantic bales of hay and one day in a country club restroom in the middle of nowhere. They welcomed us to use their facilities and have lunch. Five of us were walking together: Gabi, Laura, the young chef Matthew, David and me. Everyone had their own story. Gabi was searching for peace from a gut-wrenching family history that was defining her; Laura was anxious about leaving her mother to go away to school; Matthew was showing off how he could be a grown up at seventeen, as his parents were "done with him;" David was trying to mentor Matthew; and I was trying to leave my burdens behind and figure out the rest of my life.

Exhausted and in need of a bottle of wine, we finally made it the twenty three kilometers to Belerado. The multiple colors of the UN flags announced the albergue. We swam in the pool, and had a peregrino, or pilgrim dinner, of garlic soup, ensalada, chicken, fries and wine. A plaque on the wall announced: "The first third of the Camino is for the Body, the next third is for the Mind and the last third is for the Spirit. The Body section of the journey is complete!" Did this mean my feet wouldn't hurt anymore?

Meeting Myself

A few days later we ran into Franklin Pierce College students up on a meseta, "a table top above the world," on the road to Hornillos del Camino. They were following a maze designed by a creative pilgrim. They called it a curlicue. I probably would not have walked it myself if not for their incredible enthusiasm. As I walked in large circles my mind wandered inward to places it hadn't been before. I stayed by myself on the meseta, had lunch and thought mostly about my daughters, how they were getting on and how I could be a more positive and loving part of their lives. I sang and wondered, among many things, if I would ever experience love again. An afternoon nap came easily.

We all went back to the meseta that night and saw the Milky Way, Orion and the Big Dipper in the same sky we see at home! A brass plaque on the wall outside the San Esteban albergue was orally translated by a Camino veteran:

> "The Camino de Santiago is not a marathon or a gym. It is a bank of challenges for your humility and your real lesson in spiritual and human possibilities. The authentic Camino is

what each person does inside themselves, which means you could meet yourself and transform your life. It is necessary to understand that time is a teacher. The important equipment is your attitude of searching. Open your eyes to the beauty of the countryside and art. To those who give you hospitality with generosity, offer them gratitude."

My mind was racing trying to write down each word and contemplate their meaning. I read it each day for the rest of the journey. How much time would it take? Would I know when my life was starting to change? For the better? I needed to spend more quiet time writing in my journal and contemplating life, or at least the message in the plaque. The passing of time has made me question how I spend my days and hours. Time will slip away if I don't use it wisely. It was seriously time to slow down. What was worthy of my time?

After David went home, I had concerns about the dark mornings. I waited until other pilgrims were leaving the albergue and "offered" to walk with them. If it was a male, I had to push myself to keep up until the sun came up. After that we usually drifted apart. The solo walk for the rest of the day was now welcome and reflective. In Calsadilla de Cueza, I came upon an albergue with a pool and stopped in the early afternoon. My feet were done after sixteen kilometers that day.

ANNA

"If we have no peace it is because we have forgotten that we belong to each other."
- Mother Teresa

A pilgrim I had met a few days before had the same idea. She is a relief worker for Catholic Relief Services and had been to Pakistan and Sri Lanka helping victims after the earthquakes.

We sat with our feet in the pool that afternoon sipping wine and sharing our life stories. Sharing stories was my favorite part of the walk. In the evening I was sitting alone on a bench surrounded by sunflowers and wheat fields. The moon shared its light with me. I remember thinking about cooking more with my daughter Anna. One of my best days so far.

After a vibrant morning discussion about work and how to depersonalize the workplace, we agreed to walk in silence for the afternoon. I mostly thought about my relationship with Anna and how to improve it. I'm going to pay more attention to meals with her and their preparation. I hope this will support her busy schedule with college and work. Maybe we'll even cook together! Later that day, I found a wonderful albergue with hot showers and toilets with seats.

Day twenty two began with a panoramic sunrise of oranges, blues, and pinks. I stood looking out at the low horizon. There were distant mountains to the north overlooking the Bay of Biscay; otherwise, it was completely flat farmland. I stopped a while to rest and enjoy the scene. I could because I was walking solo!

NOBODY'S FAULT BUT MINE

With pepper spray in my pocket, I was getting used to walking alone. Then my cousin arrived. I told her about the ritual of talking for a while and then walking in silence. She thought that was a good idea, and it sort of worked while we were catching up on family news. My family had cautioned me against walking with her, not just because she's seriously independent, but her connections to people are weak.

On our third day together it happened. She abandoned me. We were walking through Astorga and she took off walking on her own. It was more than a little bit awkward. I wish she had told me and it would have been fine, but just taking off like that was disconcerting. I'm trying to be at peace with nature and myself, and this incident threw me off track. Luckily, the Camino helped. It always helps because it leads you in the right direction. I ran into another pilgrim who walked at my pace, and didn't think about "cuz" for the rest of the day. We found an oasis along the route that had food and massages. It welcomed us with a hammock and burning incense and herbs for sale. It reminded me of the sixties. People gravitated to the spot for many reasons: some were walking the Camino, some were squatting and others were farming there. The rest of the walk that day was flat and long. After showering and washing my clothes at the albergue, I found "cuz" there in the courtyard drinking beer with her new Camino friends. She yelled, "Hey, Elizabeth, come meet my new friends!"

These happened to be people I had walked with before. An unnecessary and uncomfortable competition was brewing between us. I was the one who invited her on this trip, so I had no one to blame but myself.

STONES IN MY POCKET

The next morning I rose early and let my cousin know that I was leaving for Cruz de Ferro and would see her there. While walking, I kept holding the different stones in my pocket that I picked up along The Way. These stones represented burdens that belonged to other pilgrims. The ritual on the Camino is to think about your burdens as you walk. Hold a stone for each burden in your hand and when you're ready to ask for help carrying a burden, you can put the stone on three foot pillars placed along The Way. As other pilgrims pass by, they will pick up your burdens and carry them for you to Cruz de Ferro, a cross at 5,000 feet, the highest point on the Camino. By now, I had other people's burdens in each pocket and wondered who had mine. When I arrived at Cruz de Ferro that day, it was the 28th day of my journey. I placed these stones at the foot of the cross along with my written burdens and ran down the hill. Physical and emotional lightness engulfed me the second my burdens left my hands. The rest of the hike that day was resplendent!

New Beginnings

Now with my burdens behind me, I could focus on the future. I had ten days left to ponder: "What will be important in my new life?"

A sign appeared. There was a board for each destination:

- Roma 2475 Kilometers
- Jerusalem 5000 Kilometers
- Santiago de Compostela 222 Kilometers

On to Santiago!

Day thirty one I climbed to O'Cebreiro with heavy feet and heavy pack. It took me all day! In order to take a rest I had to climb over mounds of dirt and bushes just to sit down. There were many rests. I felt like an old lady that day, but the trip was worth it. The views were consuming, mountains and farmland and windmills as far as I could see. Shades of blue and orange drew the sunset closer.

O'Cebreiro is home to the oldest church in Spain. Ironically, it had a PowerPoint in four languages to follow the hymns. Hymns are my way of praying. Peaceful wonderful evening. The walk down the next day was difficult, but the grass was green and the playful goats were entertaining. Near the bottom, the sun was out and there were scattered clouds but it was comfortable. I was definitely in the Galicia region, the final leg of the pilgrimage. The villages were small and quaint, lots of farm animals and their aroma. A dirt track led the way. Mountains are gone, and replaced with rolling hills. A camera could not capture this beauty, only the heart. I was walking solo and feeling the power. I had no idea where my cousin was. She left early this morning and I never saw her again. Sometimes problems actually do solve themselves. My daughter Meg was to arrive in a few days when I got to Sarria. The Spirit portion of the Camino had begun.

The joy of spending 24 hours a day with an adult child awakens your heart and soul. We walked on tree covered dirt paths in perfect Galicia weather and caught up on her plans for law school and my experiences on the Camino. Farm animals traveled the same paths and a herd of cattle approached us. I panicked. There was no place to go. The herder told us to stay still and let the cows go around us. Even in Spanish, I understood that instruction. Trying to remember that cows won't hurt you while their 1500-pound sweaty bodies are rubbing up against you on all sides is near impossible. The rest of the day was uneventful. We stayed in a 14th century monastery without glass in the windows that night. It was raining. I was looking for a hot cup of tea but instead was offered a bottle of wine which we passed among strangers. Sleep came easily that night.

The next day as we were walking there was an unfamiliar scent. It was a Eucalyptus farm. Perfect straight lines of trees and a beautiful aroma. We stayed awhile to ponder.

The outskirts of Santiago de Compostela looked like an average Franco era style city, with white pedestrian stucco apartment buildings and red clay roofs. Saint James cathedral was inside the walls of the old city. It's 246' high and 230' wide, with a striking blend of Romanesque, Gothic and Baroque style architecture which represented the year of each addition. I entered with a sense of accomplishment and wonder.

Yes, I had just walked 500 miles. It had taken 38 days.

Was I a different person? Did I find the meaning of life? Would I know how to proceed? I didn't ask myself these questions on that last day. I was relieved and excited to finish walking and to get that pack off my back.

Meg and I sat and took in the ritual during the noon celebration of the Pilgrim Mass and received our final blessing. We showed our Camino passport and received our certificate of completion, known as the Compostela, at the Pilgrim Office. We stayed in a former Camino hospital in Cathedral Square, which had been renovated by the Spanish Paradores. The luxury was appreciated.

THE OUTCOME

Solvitur ambulando
'It is solved by walking'
"The authentic Camino is what each person does inside themselves which means you could meet yourself and transform your life. It is necessary to understand that time is a teacher."

It turns out my Camino had three purposes. Proving myself through physical endurance. Proving myself by letting go of my burdens. And the less tangible purpose of figuring out the future of my life.

As I walked slowly through the wall surrounding the old city of Santiago the cathedral burst into view and I knew my life was entering a new chapter. The past just seemed to melt away. I was tired but felt like celebrating.

On the Camino I did meet myself and realized that I'm in charge. However, coming to that realization and living every day as this new person are two entirely different things. I have a long history of habits and feelings that define me and a posse of family and friends who are familiar with that me. Trying to change within this environment has been uncomfortable.

Upon arriving home from the Camino I immediately went back to work. Lynn and David and I had a big Camino party within a week of me touching down in Boston. I returned to my regular routine except for presentations about the walk at the local churches and libraries. I was still walking regularly but change was coming more slowly than I expected.

Writing about my journey years later is creating more understanding and thought than I experienced during the walk. Partly because my body was still vulnerable to the daily walking and partly because I wasn't used to contemplating life. I am still seeking a deeper meaning to my life.

More and more each day I am treating my experiences with intentionality and love. I am enjoying my daughters who are pursuing their own dreams, and doing a fabulous job! I want to love my new husband with my whole heart and attention. I want to enjoy my retirement and not schedule every minute. I will never again say that I am too busy. I'm prioritizing my time according to those things that are worthy of my time, such as a long walk by myself or with a friend, skyping with my grandson or...writing this very story.

May 11, 2018

GILLIAN MARY AGUILAR

Author's Note: This memoir is dedicated to my children, Bruce, John, Kim and Anne-Marie, and their respective spouses, and to my grandchildren, Benjamin, Jade, Isabella, Lily, Leah, Vaughn and Gemma. And to the memory of my beloved husband, Francis Joseph Aguilar (1932 – 2013).

A Memoir

TERROR FROM ABOVE:

"Wake up, wake up, Gillian!" My mother was shouting, and then I heard the siren wailing. I knew I had to get out of bed right away and that my mother would carry me down to the dug-out shelter at the bottom of the garden. It was 1940, a year after the start of WWII and I was three years old. As we raced down the garden, I saw my father running ahead of us holding my seven year old brother's hand. We all climbed into the dugout and scrambled into our little narrow bunks and pulled down the mosquito netting.

I don't remember what the walls were made of, just that the mosquitos were rampant. I did drift off to sleep until suddenly I woke up to hear the All Clear signal. We all breathed a sigh of relief and my brother and I turned our little cards hanging over our bunks from red to green. Holding our flashlights, we returned to the house for a few more hours of sleep. I remembered to take my Mickey Mouse gas mask with me in case we were woken up again in the night.

During the war, we lived in Pinner, Middlesex, which was part of Greater London where the bombing was most intense. Later, a German Doodlebug would explode only two miles from our house. The scary thing about those bombs was that as long as you could hear their engines up in the sky, you knew they would not come down on you. If, however, you saw one up there and didn't hear anything, it meant it was about to drop down! The wartime bombing was perhaps the most vivid memory of my childhood. I am still terrified of thunder storms and cannot easily tolerate guns being waved around on stage. It took me until age 60 to enjoy a fireworks show!

In the summer of 2017, my son John and his family spent a week in England. Whilst staying in London, John was intrigued by my stories of the dug-out shelter. So he took a train from London to Pinner, and using maps on his phone found his way from the station to North House, 6 North Way, where I spent my childhood. He knocked on the door and a very nice lady invited him into the house. He asked her about the bunker at the bottom of the garden and she told him that just last year they had had it removed. Apparently It was made of concrete and had to be jackhammered out. She even went down to the cellar to fetch the deed of the house which was made out to my father's third wife, Esme.

TERROR FROM WITHIN:

Unfortunately, my father was an alcoholic and this affected his behavior which could be quite unpredictable. I still remember his beating me with a black Army cane because I threw a candy wrapper on the ground and didn't pick it up right away. Also, he often came home at night very drunk. One night, my mother was so scared she came and locked herself with me in my bedroom. She knew my father had a revolver under his mattress and she was very frightened. When he came banging on my door, I was so scared that I tried to jump out of the second story window onto the flagstone terrace below. Luckily, my father withdrew at that moment and everyone went back to bed. The next day, my father gave me a present of atonement—a large multi-use penknife—a rather incongruous gift under the circumstances! But he was not always violent. In fact, every Sunday morning we would walk together to the local pub. He would seat me on the bench outside and bring me an orangeade and for himself a big black Guinness with lots of froth on top. He would always say: "This is the blackest Guinness you have ever seen!" I don't really remember harboring any strong resentment against him. When he finally left the family and went off with his secretary when I was thirteen, I still stayed in touch with him and sometimes met him for lunch in London.

TERROR AT NURSERY SCHOOL:

When I was four years old, I used to walk down the street to a little nursery school called Mrs. Verdon's. There was a colorful train there that I loved to play with. One day, I hid it under my coat and ran home with it. "You can't keep it," said my mother, "you will have to take it back to school." I was terrified that someone would see me and be very angry that I had taken it. But my mother said we should go right away and just hope nobody would see us. As we stood outside the school, I looked around, saw nobody, and ran as fast as I could up to the front doorstep, left the train there, and set off very fast for home. I can still remember how terrified I was at being caught!

MY MOTHER'S TURN TO BE TERRIFIED:

With nursery school behind me, it was time for grade school, a nice small school called the Knoll School not far from our house. Those were happy years spent roller skating up and down the sidewalk and climbing trees and building a wonderful tree house in the large oak tree at the bottom of our garden. A group of us boys and girls would climb up and down all day—my mother said she tried not to look out of the kitchen window as she was terrified one of us would fall out of the tree! No dolls or tea parties for me—I dressed in my brother's old clothes (to my mother's dismay as she liked to smock pretty little dresses); we had a great time playing mostly outdoors. When I occasionally came home in tears because the boys had tied me up to a tree and abandoned me for what seemed like hours, my mother had little sympathy for me. "If you want to play with your brother and his friends, that's what will happen to you." I even had to put up with losing my treasured war-time sweet ration when playing billiards and snooker with my big brother!

A Terrifying Head Mistress:

At age ten, I passed the entrance exam to St Helen's School in Northwood, where I would graduate at age 17. I hated the shapeless pea-green tunic with a beige shirt, the green and gold striped tie and ugly green blazer. There were also an unattractive green felt hat and brown lisle stockings and brown lace shoes ("no casual shoes, girls!"). The summer dress was even uglier! In clement weather, we bicycled to school about two miles along the main road. It is quite amazing that none of us was injured riding two or three abreast with cars and buses whizzing by. The one good thing about the ride was that we might be lucky enough to meet some boys from Merchant Taylors school. Of course, we were instructed by the Head Mistress not to converse with the boys! On one occasion I drew some caricatures of two of my teachers which were confiscated and given to the Head Mistress. I was called into her study and given a Black Point! That did instill terror in me. Years later I found out that the teachers had had a good laugh over my drawings! At St. Helen's I made two great friends, Linda and Margaret, who came several times to the U.S. over the years to visit.

JOURNEY INTO THE UNKNOWN:

After graduating from High School, where I had specialized in Latin, French and German, it was time for some adventure. So I packed a large suitcase and, with my mother's blessing, I set off to cross Europe by train to Innsbruck, Austria. Upon arrival, I found a room through the University housing office and enrolled in several courses. It was a great two years of skiing, speaking German and meeting up with a delightful group of Hungarians who managed to cross the border at the beginning of the Hungarian Revolution in 1956. They even gave us lessons in Hungarian and invited a group of us to travel with them for two weeks all around Italy. Today, I can still recite the national poem of Hungary (in Hungarian!) by Sándor Petőfi. In connection with my time in Innsbruck, I want to mention two wonderful friends I made there. German students were often allowed to take two semesters abroad during their years of study at university. I became friendly with a group of German students and spent a lot of time skiing and hiking with them. I spent the most time with Jutta from Kronberg, and Margret from Kaarst, and later with her husband Uli, too. In fact, many years later, when I was back in America, Margret's daughter Katrin came and spent six months with us "au pair" in order to perfect her English and learn about American customs.

BACK HOME AGAIN:

By now it was time for me to return to England and see my mother again. Armed with an Academic Translator's Diploma from Innsbruck University, I enrolled in a six-month secretarial course in English and German at St. Godric's College in London. After graduation I was fortunate to find an excellent job in the City of London with a merchant banking firm, S.G. Warburg & Company. The job was intense with letters flying out daily in English and German. I made some good friends there amongst the other secretaries, especially with one young woman named Evelyn Szilasi (a Hungarian name!) and ended up sharing a flat in London with two of them. We enjoyed lunches together every day with our very generous lunch vouchers.

TIME TO MOVE ON AGAIN:

After two years at Warburgs, it was time for a new adventure, so I packed a trunk and boarded the Queen Mary for her final voyage to New York. With excellent references from Warburgs in London, I found a job on Wall Street with their sister company, Kuhn, Loeb & Co. But I knew nobody and had nowhere to live. I knocked on the door of the Salvation Army Residence for Women but was told I would be earning too much money at Kuhn, Loeb to live there. I pleaded with them that I had nowhere to go and knew no-one in New York, so they finally let me in and assigned me to a room with a very nice young German woman. We got along very well for the few months I stayed there. New York was exciting and interesting but I decided to move to Cambridge, Massachusetts for a less harried and more peaceful life. Little did I know that life would be full of excitement there!

AN IRRESISTIBLE MAN:

In Cambridge, I was sent by the Harvard employment office to work with a famous paleontologist, Professor Movius. It was lonely up there on the fourth floor of the Peabody Museum amongst the skeletons, so on the advice of a friend I went over the river to Harvard Business School to see if there were any jobs available. Luckily, there was an opening for a secretary to the Dean of Administration and Admissions, Chaffee Hall. We got along well right from the start and I soon discovered I was working at an institution with over a thousand young men and only a handful of women enrolled in the business courses! It wasn't long before a very attractive young man appeared at my desk (having followed me across the campus, I later learned) and introduced himself as a doctoral student who was just starting to work on his thesis. What more suitable girlfriend than a young secretary who might be able to help with typing drafts of his thesis! Actually, that didn't cross my mind at the time but I did type many a draft over the next few months! It was a whirlwind courtship and Francis Joseph Aguilar (Frank) and I were married eight months later, in May of 1964 at St. Paul's in Cambridge with our reception at the Harvard Business School. My mother flew over from England to give me away. Frank was first generation American and was born in Manhattan. His father, one of a family of fifteen children, had come as a young man to America from Mexico and met Frank's mother, who had come over from Southern Germany, at an English language evening class in the city. Frank used to joke that his first language was broken English.

AN UNFORGETTABLE MOMENT:

Frank and I found a small apartment in Cambridge near the river and while he pursued his doctoral studies, I enrolled at Harvard to complete my A.B. in Extension Studies. In June of 1965, I was sitting in Harvard Yard in my simple black graduation robe when the parade of professors in their fancy and colorful robes and hoods marched by. To my great surprise and delight, Frank left the line of professors, walked over to where we would-be graduates were sitting on the stands and planted a wonderful kiss on me and then caught up with the line of professors again. I was completely taken aback and everyone around me gasped. It is one of the most beautiful memories of my life and always brings tears to my eyes.

STARTING A FAMILY:

On December 16, 1965, Bruce Crawford Aguilar was born, a healthy baby weighing 7 pounds, 12 ounces. We wrapped him in a white blanket and tied it with a big red bow and placed him under the Christmas tree! Frank was now a full professor and teaching Business Policy at HBS. We felt it was time to move to the suburbs when Bruce was several months old and would no longer fit in our dressing room in a Porta-Crib. We found an attractive stucco house in Belmont, Massachusetts, on a quiet street just a few minutes' walk from Cushing Square, which had several nice shops and restaurants. We stayed there until, in April of 1968, John Francis was born, another healthy baby, weighing 8 pounds, 6 ounces. Now we started a serious search for a larger home and found a lovely historic house on Pleasant Street just one block from Belmont Centre. It was built in 1841 in the Greek Revival style, quite popular at that time. It came with just over an acre of land, a large barn, carriage house and a small potting shed. Its location meant that we would not have to drive the children around as Belmont High School was only seven minutes' walk away and the bus to Harvard Square was one block away. The house needed a considerable amount of work, but once that was completed we sold the house on Pequossette Road and moved into our new home.

TRAVELLING AGAIN AND THE FAMILY GROWS:

My husband had just finished reading *Cheaper by the Dozen* and suggested we have twelve children so he could put into practice some of the ideas he had read about. I suggested instead that we adopt any future children as there were so many children without homes of their own. In 1972, Kim Marie, aged 4 months, arrived at Logan airport from South Korea. A few months after her arrival, the whole family set off for Lausanne, Switzerland, where Frank was to teach senior management courses for Harvard in nearby Vevey on Lac Leman. The two boys were enrolled in public school in Lausanne and were soon speaking quite good French. We decided to speak French at home, too, to help them get immersed in the language. As French was Kim's first language, she had to learn to speak English when we returned to the U.S. two years later, and John had to learn to read in English! We decided to take a year's sabbatical before returning to the U.S., "une année de recyclage."

As the whole family was now immersed in French, we set off to find somewhere in France (cheaper than Switzerland) where we would enjoy living. We settled upon Megève, France, a delightful little ski village in the Haute Savoie with about 5,000 inhabitants. We rented a chalet right in the village itself, bought season ski passes, found a lovely au pair to help us with Kim, and spent a lot of time outdoors. Frank even had a piano brought up the mountain and took lessons from the local music teacher. I helped with the school children's swimming lessons at the indoor pool and also took groups of the younger students down the mountain. With friends coming to visit from England, Germany and the U.S., and ski trips to the Vallée Blanche in Chamonix, it was a wonderful year!

HOME AGAIN!

Back in Belmont, Massachusetts, where we had rented out our large Greek Revival house on Pleasant Street during our stay abroad, we settled back into life in the U.S. English was now our preferred language. Frank went back to teaching at Harvard and the boys returned to their respective American schools and getting used to a different culture. Kim picked up English quite quickly thanks to the help of a bilingual babysitter from Belmont High School and she was soon ready for nursery school.

ONE MORE ADDITION TO OUR FAMILY:

In 1983, we adopted five-and-a-half year old, Anne-Marie, also from South Korea. Being an older child coming from an orphanage, it was a much more difficult transition than when Kim arrived as a little baby. She went to the local elementary school and had a special tutor for the first few months to help her transition from Korean to English. She had spent three years prior to her arrival in the U.S. at a very nice orphanage in Seoul, which we all visited on a later trip to South Korea. It was wonderful to see the children singing the same songs to us that Anne-Marie had learned as a little girl.

GILLIAN TAKES A JOB:

In 1985, I enrolled at Tufts University to get my Master of Arts in Teaching. Upon graduation I found a job teaching German and French at Belmont High School and also at two adult groups at home, one evening of German and one evening of French. The children were not altogether happy to have their mother at the High School although it could be quite handy when they forgot their lunch money!

MORE FAMILY TRAVELS AND THEN AN EMPTY NEST:

The years went by with many opportunities to travel because of Frank's affiliation with Harvard and their wanting teachers to give business courses all over the world. We went to several European countries, the Philippines, China, Japan, South Korea and all around Latin America. The years flew by and before we knew it, the boys were graduating from High School. They both ended up going early admission to Dartmouth College, graduating in Philosophy and Government respectively. They continued on to graduate school. Bruce is now a Chaplain at Spaulding Rehab in Boston and Cambridge and married a young lady from Brazil named Eneida. Together they have a son, Benjamin, who is now eighteen years old and preparing for college. John is a reporter for the *Denver Post* in Colorado. He met and married Jennifer while in graduate school and they have twin daughters, now fourteen years old, named Isabella and Eliana (Lily). Kim majored in Religion at Trinity College and has worked in advertising in Seattle and in a large accounting firm in Portland, Maine, near to where she now lives in Cape Elizabeth. She had three children with her second husband: Jade aged 16, and twins Leah and Vaughn, 14-years-old. Anne-Marie spent one semester at the University of New Hampshire and then set off on her own to the West Coast. For a few years we lost touch with her. However, when Frank was very ill, she came home for Christmas in 2012 and was reunited with the family. She has since become very interested in medicine and has been studying to become a Physician's Assistant. She has passed all her exams with flying colors. She is living in the lovely "City of Roses," Portland, Oregon with her husband, Woody, and new baby, Gemma, born in June of 2017. She is taking a break from her studies to care for her baby daughter but hopes to return to college later on and complete her Masters.

HAPPY MEMORIES OF SQUAM LAKE:

I should mention here that in 1982 we bought a house with five and a half acres of land on Squam Lake in Holderness, New Hampshire, where the whole family spent many weeks each year enjoying boating, sailing, windsurfing, hiking and golfing in the spring, summer and fall, and skating, skiing and mountain hiking in the winter. It was a wonderful place for the family to gather and we have many happy memories of our time spent there. In the summer, blueberries were abundant thanks to Frank's constantly cutting back brush and exposing the hidden bushes to air and sunlight. Everyone, including guests, was put on picking duty and our freezer was always full of boxes of blueberries that lasted almost into the following picking season. There were even enough for our neighbors to pick to their hearts' content!

RETIREMENT AT LAST!

In our retirement, Frank and I spent a great deal of time up at the lake. It was a lot of work keeping the property in good shape, but many happy years were spent there. Several years before Frank died, in February of 2013 at the age of 80, we had deeded the property over to the children. However, after Frank's death, they felt they did not have the time to take care of it properly with their busy lives working full time and having only a few weeks of vacation a year. So the property was sold later in 2013 to a very nice young family from Boston.

HIKING IN THE WHITE MOUNTAINS:

One of my most vivid memories is of climbing all the Four Thousand Footers of New Hampshire in both winter and summer. This was not my idea, but rather Frank's! He was born in New York City and was inspired when he first set foot in the Great Outdoors. I was always given the opportunity of going along or staying home and of course I always went along, even when the weather was freezing cold or boiling hot! I'll always remember that on one occasion I started up the mountain with my heavily laden frame pack for a long weekend of hiking with the purpose of "bagging" 4 or 5 peaks. In order to accomplish this goal, we would lug up a mountain tent, sleeping bags, light weight stove, and packaged dry food so that we would not have to descend the mountain in the evening and then go back up again in the morning. After climbing for about thirty minutes and realizing how much further there was to go, I started crying and said I couldn't do it after all. Frank did not say a word; he simply removed the pack from my back, put it on his front (he was carrying an even heavier pack on his back) and started climbing up again. After a few minutes, I pulled myself together, climbed up to where he was, and took back my pack. As it turned out, it was a very nice and productive weekend.

MOVING TO PORTSMOUTH, NH, AND REMEMBERING OLD FRIENDS FROM BELMONT:

In 2008 with all the children gone, we sold the large house in Belmont and downsized to a lovely two-bedroom condo on the Piscataqua river in Portsmouth, New Hampshire. It was difficult to leave familiar ground where I had been very active both in town politics and local activities. It was especially difficult to leave behind two very special friends, Ethel and Merry. I had met Ethel daily for about twenty-five years to walk our dogs before work. We always chatted non-stop the whole time and enjoyed our daily outing; with Merry, there were lunches and walks, too, and usually a weekly outing to a movie and sometimes a game of bridge at one of our homes. A week before leaving for our new home in Portsmouth, both Ethel and Merry gave a lovely farewell luncheon for me, inviting all the friends I had made over the years in Belmont.

In Portsmouth, I again made two very special friends, June and Jane. June has been my neighbor across the hallway all these years and I nickname her "Saint June," because she is always there for me if I need help. We often walk together before breakfast all over Portsmouth and environs and sometimes end up enjoying breakfast together at a little local eatery nearby. I was introduced to Jane at an event at *Strawbery Banke Museum*; she is also from England and loves roses, as do I. In fact, every spring we prune and clean up all the rose bushes at the Banke and keep an eye on them right through the blooming season.

Frank and I spent five very happy years enjoying all that Portsmouth had to offer before Frank's death from gallbladder cancer in February 2013. When he was first diagnosed with cancer, he was given a maximum of 6 months to live. But he found an excellent doctor at Dana Farber Cancer Institute in Boston, Dr. Charles Fuchs, the head of the G.I. department, and lived for three and a half happy and productive years, teaching business in the Extension program at Harvard and enjoying all his usual activities.

FAMILY REUNIONS:

For the past three years, the family has come together each summer for a family reunion. This year, once again, we are planning a week on Cape Cod for fifteen people! The only person who will not be with us is my brother, Christopher, whom I mentioned at the beginning of this memoir. He used to come every year from England to spend three weeks with us at Squam Lake. He died three years ago and is always sorely missed by all of us and our friends.

A LONG LOST HALF SISTER FOUND!

I had known for years that my father had had a baby girl with his second wife, Lillian. Recently, I had found out more details about her through the internet and had even managed to get in touch with her via Skype at her home in Portugal. In June of 2017, I flew to London where I met for the first time my half-sister Celia and her husband Kelvin. It was a lightning trip with time only for dinner and breakfast together. I was delighted to finally find her and enjoyed very much the short time we had together. Her mother is now 98 years old and still lives in a house with stairs to her bedroom! Celia told me she tried to get back to England once a month for a few days to visit both her mother and her husband. It was very exciting and enjoyable to finally meet her and we have stayed in touch ever since.

TWO MORE REUNIONS:

I went on to Sussex to spend two days each with my dear old school friends, Linda and her husband, Simon, who had worked very hard to make a beautiful garden behind their new house, and to Chichester to spend a couple of days with Margaret and her husband Michael. In the evening, we went to Chichester Cathedral to hear the delightful boys choir singing. Then back to Heathrow airport to fly on to Germany. Three days were spent with Jutta from my Innsbruck days at her lovely retirement home not far from Frankfurt. To my delight, Margret, Uli and Katrin drove down from Kaarst to Kronberg to have dinner with us at a very nice restaurant in an imposing old castle. Apparently, Queen Victoria had stayed there several times!

I feel I have been greatly blessed with a wonderful husband, four delightful children, seven loving grandchildren, wonderful friends, and...good health, which has allowed me to be active all my life.

KARINA QUINTANS

Author's Note: In July 1977, my family moved to Saudi Arabia. My father had received a job with a large engineering and construction firm. The project was to build an industrial city from what was a tiny fishing village on the eastern coast of Saudi Arabia—Al Jubail. To this day, this project is known as one of the largest infrastructure projects ever undertaken in the world.

Our mid-summer arrival gave us a few weeks to get settled and familiar with our surroundings before school began. We moved into a gated compound where only expats (foreigners) lived, and began adjusting to the desert heat, and Thursdays and Fridays as our weekend.

But more novel was the "such is life in Saudi" way of life— learning the myriad rules of living in the most conservative Muslim country in the world. Religious practices. Dress codes. Public Behavior. Freedom. For instance, during the Islamic holy week of Ramadan, no one could eat or drink in public. There were no churches for a Catholic Filipino family such as ours to attend on Sundays since the practice of any religion other than Islam was illegal. Women had to be wardrobe sensitive, always covering arms, legs, and ankles and avoiding tight clothing. Our moms couldn't drive, nor could they work, except in the school.

Public displays of affection weren't permitted between men and women, whether married or not. For males, it was forbidden to mingle or talk with single females.

Then there was getting used to the lack of anything American. Most western consumables, if any, were from Great Britain. There was soda but instead of Coke, Orange Fanta, and Sprite, there was Pepsi, Mirinda, and Teem. If you preferred Coca Cola over Pepsi, you were outta luck. At the time, the Arab League had imposed a ban on the sale of Coca Cola in Saudi because the product was sold in Israel. Of course, there were no pork products nor alcohol—both forbidden in the Muslim culture.

There were also no malls, movie theaters or book stores. There was no nightlife for anyone, and especially not for the hundreds of expat men on "single status" (bachelors or married without family in country). Single expat women were not allowed in the country. Deprived socially, men on "single status" were allotted more vacation time outside of the country than those on "family status."

Outside of our compounds, during evening outings to shop downtown, we were most vigilant about the rules. We moseyed about town always looking out of the corner of our eyes for Saudi's religious police—the enforcers of Sharia law known as the *mutawah*. All the while, putting up with the stares and hisses of local men; or occasionally our private parts being touched in passing. I wouldn't say we got used to all of this. It was just part of life in Saudi. Even if we complained, we'd likely be blamed for what happened. Like the stories of Filipino maids thrown in jail because they had been raped and impregnated by their Saudi employers. Somehow, it was their fault.

My apprehension about moving to Saudi was clearly not baseless. I was a ten-year-old and it just sounded scary. But over time, we settled into a rhythm. And I surprisingly came to love our life in Saudi. Mostly because of friends. Friends with whom I spent every free minute, as we watched an industrial city rise from the sands along the beautiful Persian Gulf. Friends with whom I compared notes about the cool vacations our families took to Europe, Africa, and Asia, and what new American trendy clothing we had come back with after our annual "turnarounds" back to the states. Friends with whom I snickered over who was going with whom and who made out at the last party while slow dancing to Led Zeppelin's *Stairway to Heaven*. All of this fun rooted within a daily dose of cultural experiences, both local and international.

To people back in the states, our life in the most conservative Muslim country sounded incomprehensible, even strange. And it was—on the surface. But the reality was, our expat life was rich with culture, adventure, fun, and deep friendships. We made so much of the little we had in late 70s Saudi.

So, in the spring of 1980, when my dad announced that we were moving on to a new project in a different country, my heart sank. How could I possibly leave my friends? But this was also part of life in Saudi. People came and people left the project every year.

On my last day in country, my closest girlfriends—Annika, Seana, Shelley, and Cynthia came over for the goodbye ritual we had come to know well, but still felt like the end of the world every time. We gathered. We cried. We hugged.

And then we bid goodbye.

I'VE DRAFTED MANY VIGNETTES of my time in Saudi. For this anthology, I chose to share a few short stories about "such is life in Saudi." A sort of unspoken mantra to explain away the challenging aspects of living in the most conservative Muslim country in the world in the late 70s. The stories and memories are less than savory. Nonetheless, I would do anything to go back to Saudi. To feel its intense heat, put my toes in the sands of the Persian Gulf, to eat shawarma, endlessly, and to get to know the country in a whole new way. And I plan to, as its conservative doors slowly begin to open under the rule of Crown Prince Mohamed bin Salman.

Khobar Nights

DOWNTOWN AL KHOBAR WAS CROWDED. Come nightfall, empty streets came alive with people in the Kingdom of Saudi Arabia. It was time to shop and enjoy being out and about without the intense rays of the desert sun beating down on our heads. Like a pet dog gleeful at being set free in the backyard, we jumped into dad's white four-door, excited for a little downtown adventure.

We had just moved to Saudi a few weeks earlier. For mom and dad, Saudi was old hat. They had spent four years in Saudi in the mid-60s. Nothing about it fazed them. My brother, sister, and I, on the other hand, left the states reluctantly. But the novelty of life in Saudi quickly replaced our angst with curiosity. Everyday felt like an adventure filled with new experiences and things to learn. The local people, the food, the clothing, the customs, the rules. This was geography class—in real-time. Even Dhahran Academy, a school filled with expat kids from around the world, sounded like fun. School would start soon where my brother Chik would go into 9th grade, I'd start 6th grade, and my sister Dina, 3rd grade.

Parked in a lot at the edge of the main thoroughfare, we exited the freezer-box air-conditioned car. Even in the dark of the night it was still warm, the air like the heat of a baking oven just turned off. Arms bumped arms as we weaved through crowds of people on the streets of downtown Al Khobar. Expats with their collared shirts, khakis or chinos, t-shirts, and long skirts, shuffled past the flap of white thobes and black abayas (ankle-length robe-like garments) worn by Arabs. Here and there, expat women wore kaftans—full-length, shapeless cotton dresses—to hide their bodily curves from the eyes of males. And perhaps, to avoid "the pinch" that quick little squeeze of a female expat buttocks by curious Arab male hands. To this, most expat women would simply glare or sneer in response, and then carry on. It just wasn't safe to fight back. The repercussions were risky, given the local culture. And never in our favor as foreigners.

The smells of a hot and crowded, dusty downtown—there were many! Body odor and heavy perfumes. Cigarette smoke and incense. Urine and car exhaust. But then we happened upon the scrumptious whiff of shawarma, floating through the air like a fine mist. A delight to our senses, we followed our noses in search of the rotating vertical spit on which long strips of stacked lamb, roasted slowly. Shawarma sandwich was our first love of Arab cuisine: lamb thinly sliced off the vertical spit from top to bottom, juices dribbling down, then layered with pickled radish, onion, a lemon-tahini sauce, and wrapped in fresh Arabic bread (slightly leavened flatbread).

We stepped into a grocery store, and while mom and dad shopped for food, my brother, sister, and I explored. Goods were stacked high and haphazardly throughout store's aisles, nooks and crannies. We searched for candy, music, and magazines. Anything kin to American products. But instead of M&Ms— there were Smarties; instead of a 10 Grand Bar—the Lion Bar. All British products. Once, we did find a few-months-old Time Magazine in the racks. We flipped through its pages finding sections blacked out with thick marker. Saudi's religious police, the *mutawah*, had manually censored content that violated their rules, like photos of females with bare arms or legs.

After a bit of wandering around, dad came looking for us with an air of urgency.

"Kids, head back to the car and wait there while mom finishes shopping."

"Why?"

"The *mutawah* are out. Just go now."

He handed us the keys and the three of us went straight to the car. There we sat, the car windows open, rocking out to Aerosmith on the cassette player. Safe and at ease, we waited patiently for mom and dad to return.

In the brief time we had lived in Saudi, we had learned to fear the *mutawah*—the enforcers of Saudi's public norms of behavior and dress. Stories of unlucky encounters filtered quickly through the expat community. The *mutawah* were especially prolific downtown just before and during the Islamic holy time known as *Ramadan*. They would spray women's ankles with black paint if they weren't sufficiently covered, or lightly whack their legs with a stick if their jeans were too tight.

It was local customs like these, among other worries, that bothered us when dad had told us we were leaving New Jersey to move to Saudi. We whined. *Saudi Arabia? Will we have to wear veils? Where will we go to school? Will we make any friends? What is there to DO there?*

We weren't happy with the news. We loved our five-bedroom chalet-style home with wall-to-wall shag carpeting, and our classic American childhood. We walked to school, jump-roped during recess, rode bikes in the neighborhood, played in the woods, ate at McDonalds, and watched afterschool TV shows. What we would do in Saudi?

A few days later, the three of us staged a strike. Holding signs while marching around the house, we chanted, *We don't want to go! We don't want to go!* But dad wouldn't budge. Our protest had fallen on deaf ears.

SIDE 1 OF THE AEROSMITH TAPE ENDED. Chik popped it out, flipped it over, and inserted it back into the car cassette player to play Side 2. And finally, mom and dad came back to the car, arms full of groceries. They piled the bags into the trunk, and got in to the front seat. Dad put the keys in the ignition to start the car.

"So dad, what was with the *mutawah* tonight?" asked Chik.

"Some expats told me that the *mutawah* were all over downtown grabbing men with long hair. They were taking them to a room somewhere to shave off their hair, and then let them go," dad explained in a *such-is-life-in-Saudi* matter of fact voice.

"Geez...glad I came back..." Chik snickered as he shook his head, as if to double check—his signature American 70s-style, long, feathered hair, still there.

Unemptied Pockets

American goods were largely absent in late 70s Saudi Arabia. No Coca Cola, no Bubble Yum, no books, no posters, no television shows, no clothing. Music was one thing we *could* get. In bootleg form. Often poorly recorded, album songs were strangely re-ordered or omitted. Sometimes music from other albums was tacked on the end to fill space. Like foreign newspapers and magazines, cover art was subject to redaction with the black marker if inappropriate. We didn't care. Music was our thing, our collections a point of pride. *Who has Rush 2112? How about Aerosmith's Draw the Line?* Daily, we sat for hours on street curbs and corners, happily blaring 70s rock from our boom boxes. And at night, during house parties, we played 70s disco and slow-danced to Led Zeppelin's Stairway to Heaven. We were constantly copying and making mixed tapes for ourselves and each other.

In search of new music, my friends and I took the fifteen-minute shuttlebus ride into town. Our pockets filled with Saudi riyals, we walked into the store, excited to spend. Unlike the poster-filled walls of music stores back in the states, this Saudi store was barren, as were most stores in late 70s Saudi. Poster-less walls were sand-colored and the floors dusty and dirty. Towards the back, a long glass case held bootleg tapes. Two young Saudi men in their *thobes* and *ghuttras (red and white checkered head wrap)* stood behind the case ready to make sales.

Swarming the store, Annika, Roddy, Steve, Paul, Cynthia, Seana, and the rest of us looked around. Eager to find music by Rush, Aerosmith, Ted Nugent, Led Zeppelin, Styx, Journey. Or any Western or American music, really.

Wearing a light cotton fitted t-shirt, I walked to the glass case and leaned, my chest just above counter level. I looked down to scan the collection of tapes. But after a few seconds, I felt the glare of eyes on me and I began to feel uncomfortable. I glanced up and briefly met eyes with the Arab guy directly on the other side of the glass case. He stared intently at me like a cat ready to pounce on its prey. My eyes darted down.

Suddenly, he reached across the glass case and gently pinched my nipple. In scorn, I noted his creepy smile.

I looked down again into the glass case full of cassettes, as if nothing had happened. *Leave me be—I'm here to buy tapes! PLEASE be done misbehaving!* I thought to myself as I looked on. I really wanted to look at tapes. But I was distracted and tense. I saw nothing. I looked in vain.

Boom! Out reached his hand again. Pinch!

My adrenaline spiked. I looked up again. His smile was bigger. Wider. Almost prideful. His eyes dancing in triumph.

Extremely annoyed, I quietly and calmly turned away from the glass case, not wanting to provoke more of his attention. I milled about aimlessly, avoiding eye contact with the guy, feeling anxious to leave.

It wasn't long before everyone was done shopping. We filed out of the store. And true to *"such-is-life-in-Saudi,"* I bit my lip, and in silent anger boarded the bus and returned home empty-handed. My pockets still filled with Saudi riyals.

Not #MeToo

LIKE EVERY DAY IN SAUDI, the desert sun was raging this Friday afternoon, the holy day and last day of the weekend. Mom and dad were away at a teachers conference in Nepal, and I was staying with the family of my 8th grade best friend, Shannah. I didn't care about going to Nepal. It was my last spring vacation in Saudi. Come summer, we were moving to South America, and I wanted every day possible with my friends.

Other than mealtime these past couple of years in Saudi, my friends and I were always together. Stripped of our American lives, our togetherness was a way of coping with our barren surroundings. We were together on the school bus. Together in class. Together in afterschool swim meets and at weekend parties. Together in the streets with our boom boxes playing 70s rock. Together at beach bonfires, or the new Rec Center, eating burgers, playing pool, foosball, racquetball, and squash. And, together after dinner doing more of the same. We even snuck out after midnight to be together again.

"Who's going out *tonight tonight?*"—our code for sneaking out after midnight.

"Come get me!" I'd say to a couple of my guy friends. After sleeping a couple hours, I'd wake up to my alarm, slap on my clothes, then pop into my sister's bedroom to let her know. Back in my room, I would peer out the window every few minutes waiting for Roddy, Steve, Mero, Rick or Russell to come get me. My heart raced in anticipation of the soft *knock knock* on my window, the wire screen muffling the sound in the still of the night. I'd open the window and look around for the security guards. They'd make nightly rounds, street by street, looking for nefarious behavior by outsiders. Once the truck left the cul de sac, I'd jump out the window, and off we'd go to do more of the same. Hang out. It was so much fun. With only a few months left in Saudi, I was so glad mom and dad let me stay behind with friends. I couldn't get enough my friends.

WITH NO ONE OUT AND ABOUT yet in the midday heat, I decided to go home to do a few things.

"I'm going back to my place for a while to get some clothes... do a few things," I said to my hosts.

Once there, I kicked back, cranked some music, and grabbed a snack without a bother.

Until a knock at the door interrupted my peaceful afternoon.

I opened the inside door and popped open the screen door to a man standing before me. He was about 5'10" with a lanky build, and a head of short brown hair. He wore a golf shirt with different colored stripes, and a pair of knee-length shorts and leather sandals. His face was boyish and kind.

"Hi! I was next door visiting. I saw you walking home and wanted to come over and say hi," he said. Since he knew my neighbors, I let him in. He stood at the doorway to the family room. I leaned on the arm of the couch keeping some distance between us.

"Where are your parents?" he asked, tentatively.

"They're in Nepal for a teachers conference. I'm staying with friends on 40th Street. I came home to get some clothes and listen to some music for a while."

He shrugged, suddenly seeming antsy.

"Can I...Can I kiss you?" He took a small step forward.

My body stiffened.

"Ummm...I don't think so," I said calmly and without hesitation. Thoughts began to float above my head like speech balloons in a comic strip—*deportation...jail...what's this guy thinking?!...I know it's hard...hey guy, you know better!*

Sheepish and apologetic he began to backtrack.

"I'm sorry...I've been here for six months. There are no single women around. I am starting to go crazy. I saw you walk by... You're so pretty...I just thought, maybe, maybe we could share some affection...I...I'm sorry...I will leave you alone."

He swayed back and forth a bit, his body still wanting.

"You should go," I urged lightly.

"OK, I will. I...I'm sorry, I'm so sorry." Like a dog with its tail between his legs, he turned and walked towards the door. I followed behind maintaining distance. He exited. I shut and locked the door.

I zoomed back to my room, threw a few clothes in my bag, turned off the music, and left in earnest. My afternoon ruined. I walked back to Shannah's house, my head in a whirlwind.

Thank god nothing happened! Shit, something COULD have happened. How'd he know I was alone?? I feel bad for the guy. It's not easy living here. I get it. Not gonna make a stink. He held back. Nothing to report. Besides. This is Saudi. Keep your mouth shut, Karina. Such is life in Saudi.

I opened the door to Shannah's house, walked into her bedroom, and plopped my stuff done. She looked up.

"So what's going on? We going out tonight tonight?"

SUSAN MCCARTHY

Almost: Two Brief Memoirs

"The motto should not be: Forgive one another;
rather, understand one another"
– Emma Goldman

FRESH MEADOWS, OFF BELL BOULEVARD

I loved my grandparent's house, loved the tiny yard, hammock, patio picnic table, patch of grass—loved the front stoop atop the long concrete flight of steps. Hot summer nights under thin, pink and white quilts on crisp iron-starch sheets. Window closed winter's bottled cooking, cigarettes and Ivory soap, mingled Taboo and Old Spice. And always in evening quiet, the ticking of the clocks. Grandma set them minutes apart, so the bells, gongs, chirps and chimes of the many clocks, tolled one after the other, each beginning in the fading wake of another. In the middle of the night, when cuckoo's last notes melted away into softest silence, I'd wait. My breath held, perfectly still, listening for the clocks to begin again, my lullaby of time.

I always looked forward to staying at my father's parent's house, days with my grandmother, evenings with them both. Though they bickered more or less constantly, there was symmetry to their lives; the house was the two of them entwined and never the same without them together. They may be long gone from this world, but in my heart and mind, I still find comfort moving through my memories of them, walking again through their front door.

She showed me how to Charleston on the soft blue carpet of their living room, my grandmother humming a twenties tune while she danced. I'd try to imitate her, elbows out, arms crossed, hands on knees, kicking forward, then back. I have a picture of her in my living room: a sepia flapper, a young woman in an Art Deco frame. She was the Belle of the ball.

My grandpa was tall, sometimes gruff. His tawny freckled skin and swept back hair reminded me of a lion. He didn't play blocks or skip rope with us like grandma did, but he took us places, and told us things. Sometimes stories about what it was like growing up, fighting over the one pair of shoes shared between him and his two brothers. The winner wore the shoes to the dance. He listened to Jerry Vale, hated Willie Nelson's braids, and loved, loved watching Benny Hill.

My grandmother would move the hands on the cuckoo clock and make the little bird sing for us, over and over. On every visit she would measure us against the inside of the cupboard door, always touching the tip of the pencil to her tongue before marking our progress. We'd clean the house before the cleaning lady came, go to the market, and do laundry in the basement, where at just the right time, a moment known only to her; she'd fling open the washer top and plunge her hands in, moving and agitating the clothes. Days at Bar Beach spent scooping up starfish, or at the cabana in the Far Rockaways. Sometimes, we'd sit and talk at the picnic table in the backyard, out in the summer sweet air, inhaling liquid green light shining through the Honeysuckle hedge, picking their warmed sweet blossoms for our mouths. And wait for grandpa to come home.

"I wanted to be a ballet dancer when I grew up," she'd told me. Reminding me why a young lady's posture was important. I don't know, or can't remember if she'd ever been to the ballet, but when I was older, I remembered that confession, and bought her a book of photographs: tulle stiff skirts and shiny pink toe shoes, all in pose. Elegant and postured like her.

Her father had died of TB when she was twelve, and she'd had to leave school, helping deliver to speakeasies the bathtub gin and wine her mother made. She held up a bottle. "This is the last bottle of Elderberry wine that my mother made, and when you're old enough, we'll open it together."

Sleep-overs usually meant a chance to go to work with grandpa. The Fiat-MG dealership with its breezy odors of leather and oil, gas and machine, was a mobile playground. We ran rampant in the showroom, gymnasts jumping on the sporty little cars. Spinning chairs till dizzy, mercilessly punching adding machine buttons, random patterns on ever growing rolls of paper snaking to the floor; and though we were such misbehaved heathens, we were always treated to McGinnis' Amusements before we'd head back to the house and grandma. Right door lunch: left door games. And in the recess between two choices, a towering glass case where the gypsy waited for coin, ready to wake in the dimly lit foyer and deal fortune in a color whirring mechanical shuffle.

In the evening we might sit in the folding lawn chairs on the front stoop or in the back, swinging on the hammock. Grandma would slide back the glass door from the kitchen, calling us to dinner. The oak table in the tiny room covered in blue and white checkered every day vinyl, bread and butter, green and red summer tomatoes. At the table I'd ask my grandfather to tell me stories about when he was young: the one room schoolhouse in Connecticut, or my favorite, the time his mother tied him to a tree as punishment for stealing a Model T from a traveling salesman, his mother and the salesman running down the road after him.

While he talked, we ate, and the sky would darken behind him, the little kitchen suspended alone in light.

MOURNING SONGS

Their house was filled with sound, a chorus of conversation. Creased, perfumed ladies moved together, bustling about, bringing trays of foods and fruits. More coffee. More cream. Clinking spoons stirred inside porcelain cups and clattered on saucers.

My grandfather had died a few days earlier, and now, after the planning and rituals were done, family, friends and neighbors gathered together in their small house. Restless, needing something to do, I began picking up stray cups and plates, stopping here and there to talk with relatives on my way to the kitchen. After loading the dishwasher, I stood for a moment, looking out at the yard through the sliding glass door, noticing my dad standing on the patio. I slid open the door to go out, then changed my mind. I closed the door, but continued watching him for a few more minutes, before turning around and walking back to the living room.

***

WHEN I WAS YOUNG, he always said he'd take me to Europe with him on one of his business trips. One of many promises my father tossed out like crumbs. But when I was sixteen, my dad finally asked. "In a few weeks, I'm going to London, then to Paris. It's a quick trip, just a few days. If you want to go with me, you can."

It was part of an event with Air France. He showed me the invitation; it was something special having to do with the Concord. I was happy he wanted to include me. Excited, cautiously hopeful, I anxiously counted down the days.

In London, we took one of the big black taxis I'd loved to the Grosvenor House, a hotel we'd visited before as a family. I remembered that pleasant hush of formality enveloping us just inside the door from wet and teaming streets, the warming pots of tea and cocoa for me and my brothers at the little tables arranged in the lobby. Bedrooms with oversized windows overlooked city streets and Hyde Park. I was glad to be there again.

We spent the afternoon shopping on Carnaby Street, where my father picked for me mod swirling skirts and dresses amid street music and bell bottoms, the colors standing vibrant against a graying sky. Laden with bags, we made our way back to the hotel without much conversation. I was content. We were having a good time together. I didn't want to say anything that might ruin our day. Silence was always safe.

We'd dined that evening with two men, business associates he said. I can no longer picture their faces, just the dark suits, wide French cuffs and shiny cufflinks. We were seated at a table alongside a paneled wall towards the far corner of the room where I was able to watch the tide of people moving in and out. I'd felt grown-up and pretty in the gauzy smocked red and gold printed dress with voluminous bell sleeves that he'd bought for me; I shook them back to take the menu handed to me by the maître de. I looked at the menu and noticed that there weren't any prices. Curious, I reached out and pulled at the corner of my father's menu and could see that his did.

"Dad, why does your menu have prices and mine doesn't?"

"Girl's menus don't have prices."

"I don't understand what..."

He cut me off, "it's not important, just look at your menu and decide what you'd like. We're talking." He nodded at the two men. They talked throughout dinner while the waiters invisibly served, poured, and cleared. I pulled into myself; there was no part of their conversation that a teenage girl could latch on to, so I fantasized about running away and living as an artist somewhere. I could be on my own. Free.

Later, the low murmur of voices woke me up. It was the middle of the night. I could hear a woman's voice coming from my father's end of the suite. I lay there in the dark, straining my ears, trying to decipher what I was hearing. Upset and unsure...I debated: should I get up? Open the door? Yell out for my dad? But in the end I stayed put, kept quiet, and eventually, tired and jet-lagged, drifted back to sleep.

Over breakfast the next morning, I asked him, "Dad, who was here last night?"

He looked up from the paper he was reading, "No one was here, you must have been dreaming."

"I know I heard someone."

"No one was here, you're imagining things."

I was going to press on, I generally did, but before I could, he got up from the table.

"I told you, no one was here!" His voice was the deep hypnotic song he used when lecturing me. "It was just a dream. I'm telling you there wasn't anybody here. You're just tired; we had a long day yesterday."

As always, the doubts began to circle in my head. Maybe I did imagine it. Maybe it was a dream. He walked to the door, "I've got to make a call. Go and lie down. Get some rest, then pack. We're leaving for the airport in a few hours."

We had one day and one night to spend in Paris. I'd never been there before and was hoping to go to the Louvre, or see the Eiffel Tower, but not too long after we'd gotten settled in the hotel, he brought me downstairs and put me in a cab. Handing me a bundle of neatly folded Francs through the open window, he told me he had a meeting. Giving the driver an address, he bent down so he could see me. "You have an appointment to have your hair done. Have fun. I'll see you back here later." Then he was gone.

The cab pulled out from the hotel's drive and joined the swarm of blaring horns and screeching tires, multitudes of tiny cars all vying for the same point in space. I hung on and watched the scenery flicker across my window.

After leaving the salon, I'd showed the hotel's card to another cab driver, and enjoyed the ride back a little more. The weather was mild and breezy, the city beautiful.

I found my dad waiting in the marble and gilt lobby going over some paperwork. He got up, stretching his long legs, "give me a minute to put this upstairs and we'll go out."

We walked for several hours, a silent stroll of winding streets, bistros, cafes and shopping. He bought me a pair of beautiful French shoes, creamy bone leather with high mahogany heels. I couldn't wait to wear them that evening.

We were having dinner with a couple that dad knew. Friends of his he said. They picked us up at the hotel and we drove to a small restaurant, a few steps down from street level, a white tiled, cozy room with two long communal tables. No menu. One course after another kept appearing. My glass was refilled each time I emptied it, Champagne, red and white. Nobody asked if I was old enough to drink. The room started to spin. The hum of French chatter and low music grew louder; the sound of forks meeting plates began to grate. It was too much, and suddenly nothing felt right, "Dad, I want to go home."

I slept like a drunk, only waking when my father came in. He leaned against the wall, his face cupped in his hand, his thinking face. "When you're packed and ready, come to my room. I need your help with something."

I couldn't imagine what kind of help he'd need from me, but I got up, dressed, and packed my things. My head was splitting. I felt sick.

I knocked on his door and walked in. He was standing next to piles of cash, neatly bundled and banded, stacked on the dresser next to a large roll of tape. He'd already begun taping some of the bundles to his torso, but needed me to walk the tape around him. For once, I did as I was told, too stunned to argue. Round and round and round. The only sound in the silence between us, the squelching sounds of tape separating itself from the roll as I circled. Faint noises from the street seemed a long way away.

When we were ready to go, he handed me my ticket and

passport: "if anyone stops me, just keep walking and get on the plane. You don't know me."

On the plane we sat separately, rows apart. I was hung over and terrified, praying nothing would happen to him. Afraid I'd somehow do something to give him away. He slept. I went through customs by myself, meeting him on the other side. I'd taken off the shoes he'd bought me, walking barefoot through the airport, exhausted, crying with relief when I saw my mother.

***

I WANDERED BACK IN TO THE KITCHEN, looking through the sliding glass door to see if my dad was still outside. He was gone. The doorbell rang and I turned and watched as a new group of ladies bearing trays came in through the front door. Kissing cheeks, and bestowing one armed hugs as they made their way to the kitchen. Clouds of tobacco smoke hung low over the groups clustered in the foyer, living room, hall and kitchen, making the air warm and close. Steam from coffee cups, held or discarded, rose up in soft spirals, and heat radiated from too many bodies too close together. I needed air.

At the top of the landing the Ivory soap air felt clear and clean, and the night light shone through the shadows. I walked the few steps across the hall into their bedroom and looked around the familiar room. Grandma's amethyst glass atomizer sat on top of her bureau next to the small container that held her mother's hairpins. A silky yellow coverlet lay over their neatly made bed, grandpa's chair close beside it.

Grandpa's big blue chair had always had a place in my grandparent's living room. It's where he sat, and where we kids perched on its wide rolled arms, though always told not to, leaning in to watch TV with him. We kissed him hello while he sat in his chair and hugged him goodbye.

Some years before he died, my grandmother had a new chair custom made for him. The old chair was temporarily banished to the basement. But grandpa refused to sit in the new chair.

Not even once. As a compromise, the blue chair was brought up to their bedroom, and there it stayed, next to her nightstand, near to his closet.

I went over and sat in Grandpa's big blue chair. I straightened out the arm covers, first the left, then the right. Then I noticed a light was on in his closet, the door slightly open.

As I moved closer, I could hear the barest whisper of sound coming from inside. I pulled the door open.

And there, sobbing alone, his face buried in an armful of shirts gathered tightly to his chest, stood my father.

I didn't know what to do. So I said nothing. And he said nothing. The opportunity to share our grief, to touch, slipped away again.

Years later when he was dying, I'd go to see him whenever he was hospitalized, sometimes going nearly every day after work. I'd bring him soup and sit in his silence for a while, near, but not close to him. Finally understanding that we'd both done the best we could.

LIZ NEWMAN

Author's Note: The following essays and poems embody my transition from anger to acceptance. This didn't happen overnight. The realization that it is futile to possess anger at someone who cannot possibly understand was freeing. I was 31 years old when I lost my first job. I went into a deep depression and sought help. I discovered that what I thought was my relatively happy life was not my idea of happiness at all.

My first epiphany came when I was reading a book called *Trapped in the Mirror*, a collection of essays by adults that had grown up with narcissistic parents. I was reading one of the essays and I burst into tears. It was the beginning of piecing my life together. I realized there was nothing wrong with me just because I wasn't meeting my mother's expectations. It wasn't because of me that I never felt safe with my father. I felt I had been cheated of a loving, supportive family. I was angry. Over time I was able to face this head on, and grieve the loss of the family I thought I had. I write these short essays and poems to share my experience and hope that it can help someone else come to the same understanding.

A Short History of Regret and Forgiveness

THE LIVING ROOM

My father often sat in the living room, leaning his chin in his hand, always his right, with his elbow on the arm of his chair. He could hold this position for hours. And somehow, his glasses were never set askew by the position of his head. He was uncommunicative when he was like this, maybe a grunt or a monosyllabic answer if asked a question. He sat with closed eyes, not sleeping, just isolated, as if a Do Not Disturb sign was hung around his neck.

He always stationed himself in the living room. A wide entryway opened to the front hallway where the stairs from the second floor landed. There were curtains on the windows that my mother had made. My father bought her the blue and white oriental rug she chose at an auction. It was the center piece of the room. She was so proud of that room. She loved that the rug and all the furniture and knickknacks were all blue and white. And there was his stereo: black and brown, displayed in a prominent position in the center of the wall, where it could not be missed. This was his stamp that marked his territory. This was his prized possession, not to be touched. Just one more barrier between us.

My father was the only one who used this room on a regular basis, usually on the weekend when everyone was home. You couldn't help but walk by that large, open entry. He had a designated armchair that was positioned so you could see him as you walked past the room. He always looked pained, as if he wanted someone to reach out to him but at the same time would push you away. He would blast opera through his stereo to shut out any noise that might disturb him. It felt like he occupied and invaded the whole house. We steered clear of that room. The louder the opera blasted from that stereo, the more tension it created. We tiptoed around, skirting that room, avoiding looking at him. He was quiet, at least, and we were afraid of setting off his anger. It was such a relief when he went out. He never told us where he was going. I'm not sure if he thought we cared.

My father and I had so much in common: our love of animals, music, our disorganized organization. I wish I'd felt safe with him. If only I could have walked into that living room and sat down in the chair opposite him. If only I could have asked: "Why did you shut me out, Dad?"

The father I wished I had, the father that every daughter deserves, would have opened his eyes, lifted his head and looked directly at me. He wouldn't have looked off into space as if I wasn't there, ignoring me as if I was an intrusion into his peace.

If only, just once, he would have said, "I love you, Liz. I didn't know you wanted to be close to me."

"If ever I tried to connect, I was afraid you would reject me. It was safer to cut you off than risk being hurt. I'm sorry that we missed out on so much that a father and daughter should share. I didn't know what else to do."

I called him after one of our many estrangements. This was the last time we spoke. I was in my early twenties and sitting at my work desk on Wall Street when I decided to call him. My intent was to invite myself over for Father's Day.

"Hi, dad."

"Nice of you to call your father."

Right off the bat he starts and I'm already angry. He hasn't spoken with me for months. Fed up with this nonsense I responded, "I'm sorry, I didn't know your fingers were broken. You could pick up the phone, too, you know. Would you rather continue this or would you rather I come over for Father's Day?"

Our reconciliation didn't last long. Communication broke down in an argument. A few years went by before I tried again, inviting him to my wedding. But eventually our pattern emerged: anger and reproaches. The last time I contacted him I tried a different approach.

Hoping to forge a more enduring relationship, I wrote him a letter. I tried to connect with him through opera, hoping it was neutral territory.

"I've recently developed a real interest in opera but I don't know where to start as far as starting a collection. Who would you suggest I buy recordings of?"

But I was rebuffed.

"You collect what you like," he responded.

I was reproached for being a daughter that did not call her father.

He declared, "I will not discuss a very painful period in my life."

"Your pain!?" I responded angrily. "What about mine? I was just a child caught between two adults at war!"

But this time it was not spoken, it was written, to be read over and over again.

The last letter I received from him began: "Listen, girlie."

And I knew. There could not be, would not be, an amicable relationship with him. I stopped reaching out to him and he never reached out to me.

It's been over twenty years.

MY OWN MEDUSA

Just a little girl, afraid to choose my clothes for the day. What if I made the wrong choice? It would mean I was not the perfect daughter. You might reject me. I would have no mother. Who would take care of me? I was devastated that I needed your help. You should have told me it didn't matter. You should have helped me pick out an outfit, not chosen one for me. It would have made such a difference. You mocked me with that story for the rest of your life, every time I panicked when I had to make a decision. You made me feel like a failure.

Older, but still just a girl, a teenager. I had to fight for my right to think for myself. That was not allowed. First came your glare of rejection, your eyes turning to ice. Then came the slap if I would not back down. All your pent-up rage exploded at me, an innocent. I was closed out from your love. I was cornered. I was forced to choose my way or your way, my thoughts or your thoughts, my needs or your needs. And you always won.

It invoked a ferocity in me I did not know I had. I would leap across the room at you, determined to demand your attention, to demand you acknowledge me as living, breathing flesh, even if injuring you was my only option. That is what you taught me. If all else fails, resort to violence.

Then, ashamed of my actions, I would beg your forgiveness. Plead with you to take me back into your arms. But you sat there, unmovable as a stone statue, silent. I could not breathe if you discarded me, a used up, dirty rag. What was I to do except bow to your demands and give up my thoughts, my needs, so that you could have yours fulfilled?

You intended to cow me and succeeded for most of my life. My twenties was a time to figure out who I was, not how to fulfill your dreams. In my forties, you no longer controlled my choices. I knew that I would never get the approval I had sought.

So, I stopped trying.

It Was More Than Just Plants

My mother loved plants. She could bring a plant back to life that most people would have given up for dead and thrown in the trash. People would bring her plants and ask her to save them. They were precious to her. Her love of plants extended to the outdoors, too. She always planted a garden wherever she lived. When she moved into an apartment building, she created a garden out front for everyone to enjoy. Passersby often stopped and told her what a lovely garden she had when they saw her outside weeding or planting.

I love to have a garden, but I'm not very good at gardening.

I like a garden that looks like a field of wildflowers. I enjoy looking at the flowers, planting them, playing in the dirt. I like hardy plants that don't need to be carefully nurtured. My mother, on the other hand, loved to see the products of her labor, to keep her hand in the process, be responsible for their flourishing.

She was better at nurturing plants than her children. She was better with plants because she could pick exactly what she wanted them to be and they gratefully responded to her care.

I always felt responsible for my mother's happiness, which is why I included her in creating my garden. After my husband and I bought our first home, I wanted a garden to replace the slope of weeds in the front of the house. I dug it all up and created a terraced slope with rock walls at each level. I was very proud of it. I invited my mother to come and help me plant.

I loved cosmos and sunflowers, she loved ground covers and petunias. Most of the time we worked in separate parts of the garden. Working side-by-side would not have gone very well. It would have taken all the enjoyment out of the task for me.

"You're not digging that hole deep enough. You're digging that hole too deep. That's too much water. That's not the way to do it, let me."

This would have been what I heard if my mother had not been focused elsewhere in the garden.

I didn't dictate what I wanted planted. It was enough that I was providing some happiness for her and anything was better than a slope of weeds in front of my new house.

But later that year we came to emotional blows.

I love cosmos. I'd planted some seeds and they were thriving. I love their tall stalks and feathery leaves with delicate-looking flowers at the top, how they sway in the wind. My mother decided she wanted to plant something where one of my clusters of cosmos had sprouted.

She started pulling them out. "They're just weeds," she said.

There was a time, even in my adult life, when I would have given into her opinion, believed my love of these plants as stupid and ridiculous. This was typical of our relationship. If it wasn't important to her, it shouldn't be important to me. But I wasn't the same person anymore.

A few years earlier, before my husband and I had bought this house, when we lived a half mile up the road from her, I'd had a telephone conversation with my mother that shut down communication between us for two years. Previous to this I had called her two to three times a day. I felt guilty if I ever skipped one call. A husband who loved me and some sage advice from a good therapist gave me the strength to stand up to her.

Larry and I had been married for six years, he'd been sober for seven. Granted, his first impression on my mother was not the greatest. He'd still been drinking. He wasn't a sloppy drunk, but he always had to have at least a beer, if not something stronger, at hand. But this was seven years later. Ever since I'd met him my mother had been dead set against him. Many conversations with my mother often included the phrase, "Elisabeth, you don't know what you're doing! He's nothing like us."

It's still a joke between my husband and me, 27 years later.

The reality behind all her comments was to undermine my marriage. After six years of this, I'd had enough.

She started complaining and denigrating Larry, repeating for the umpteenth time her disappointment when she met him for the first time. I finally said, "Give it up, mom. He stopped drinking seven years ago."

She was beyond furious.

"Don't make me choose, mom, because this time you're going to lose."

She exploded. She lost control and the next words out of her mouth were, "I should come over there and slash your throat!"

I suppose I should have been more shocked by her statement but violence in my family was nothing new. But I had come to understand that I deserved more respect than this.

"I don't have to take this anymore," and I hung up.

For two years she never picked up the phone to apologize and I had nothing to apologize for, so neither did I. We rode the same bus line into Davis Square to get the T into town. Her bus stop was after mine, so for two years if I saw her waiting for the bus, I would move to the back so that she wouldn't see me. One day, I ended up behind her on the escalator going down to the train.

"Hello," I said.

She didn't seem to recognize me at first, but then she said: "Oh, Liz."

And the next words out of her mouth were, "I've had cancer."

What was I to say to that? I did not feel guilty, as I once would have. I was angry. I had been shut out, not an unknown tactic in her repertoire.

"You could have called me anytime. I would have helped."

"Well..." was all she said.

When we got to Harvard Square she asked me if I wanted to go get a cup of coffee. We sat in Au Bon Pain while she told me what had happened with her cancer. She never asked me what I had been doing and after fifteen minutes she said she was going to the movies and had to go. I was stunned.

I sat there wondering if that was it... were we done?

The next day she called me.

"I don't know why I left like that," she stated.

I knew that it would be too easy for me to fall back into the guilt-ridden, submissive daughter, that I'd be afraid to say things that she needed to hear because it might cause her distress. I knew that I needed some kind of reinforcement, a mediator so that this conversation between my mother and I did not descend into chaos and anger.

"If you want us to have a relationship, I want us to go to a family counselor," I firmly demanded.

We didn't attend therapy for very long. In the first session the counselor asked us why we were there. I told her about the infamous phone conversation and the resultant two-year separation.

"Rosemary, why were you so angry?" the therapist asked her.

"I wasn't angry," my mother responded calmly.

Both I and the counselor sat there dumbfounded.

I confronted my mother on how she treated me growing up. She made excuses: she was very depressed, my father was a bully, she was going through menopause.

I remember just sitting there repeating the phrase, "I don't care, you shouldn't have treated me like that."

More than once my mother stood up angry and crying and said she was leaving. This was her usual response when she was confronted. But to her credit she stayed. After a few weeks of this, and the counselor repeatedly pushing her to say why she'd been so angry, my mother became hysterical again and threatened to leave.

I finally said, "if you walk out that door, we are through."

Things went a little smoother after that. There was only one more time that she had one of her "tantrums." And that was in the garden.

This was the day she started pulling the cosmos out of the ground. I tried a gentle approach.

"I like the cosmos, leave them."

"They're just weeds. They'll take over the whole garden. I want to plant something else here, it will look better," she said.

"I don't want anything else there. The cosmos stay."

This wasn't just a fight over flowers, this was a fight for my life. She walked away in a fury.

"I want to go home!" she cried.

"Why do you want to go home?" I asked innocently, knowing full well this was her response whenever I disagreed with her.

This time she came up against a Liz that she did not know. This Liz could not be cowed by hysterics and rejection.

"Mom, when you start pulling out the cosmos, flowers that I just told you I like, you make me feel like you're tossing me aside, as if I don't count for anything."

I did not finish the thought in my head: 'like you've done my whole life every time I wanted something different than you desired.'

I could only go so far. I felt this need to protect her from my truth, my experience of her. I still perceived her as fragile. When I think about it today, this woman was hardly fragile. She was divorced after twenty-five years of marriage. She worked full-time until she was 72 years old. She survived cancer twice. She launched a second career as a teacher of English as a second language in her 70's and went to Prague to teach there for six months. I knew she loved me. I also knew that my life's experience and her role in it would fall on deaf ears.

But she continued to cry and insist she wanted to go home.

"We spent weeks in therapy together so that this wouldn't happen anymore. I will take you home, if that's what you really want. But, if you walk away now instead of having this conversation, it will be the last time that you do it."

I hated having to threaten my mother with our relationship but it seemed to be the only thing she responded to.

When she was 84 she was rushed to the hospital. One medical problem after another prevented her from going home. She was back and forth between hospitals and rehabs. She had five surgeries within eight months. Her heart wasn't in good shape when all this started and after each operation a little more of her stamina ebbed away.

She asked me to take care of her plants for her while she was away. She had friends in the building where she lived whom she could have asked to do this but she asked me, her daughter. Was it her expectation that her daughter should be taking care of her that prodded her to make the request? I'm not sure. Did she consider how much I was already doing for her? Did she think about my life's situation at all? Probably not. Her apartment was in Somerville, the hospitals and rehabs she stayed in were in Boston and Cambridge. I lived over an hour away in Maine and was working two jobs. But I did it, without complaint, hoping it would give her some comfort that I was willing to do this for her.

She gave me specific instructions on how and when to water them. I watered and fed those plants as directed. I talked to them.

"Rosemary will be home soon," I would tell them.

But she'd become frail with the extended stay in hospitals. Her medical issues required increasingly specialized nursing care that could not be provided for her at home. She was old and unhappy, too weak to get out of bed by herself. She was at the end of her life.

One day I walked into her room and found her friend there visiting. She asked me how her plants were doing and then turned to her friend and said: "I know she's killing my plants."

I don't know why she said it. Maybe she was showing off to her friend, maybe she wanted me to leave because she had other company, maybe she was angry because she could not go home and was blaming me for it. It doesn't really matter why.

I visited her two to three times a week. If she had a surgery, I was there before she went in and after she came out. I talked to her every day, checked in with the doctors and nurses. I kept her informed of anything and everything that concerned her out of respect for her as a person, not just a frail, old lady. I fought like hell to get her home because I knew that was what she wanted. She was still sharp as a tack and believed she could still live independently. I set up her apartment with things that would make it easier and safer for her and some little extras. On my visits I would tell her what I had bought for her apartment. She seemed pleased.

But all she could say to her friend, while I was standing there was, "I know she's killing my plants."

HER BROWN SHOES

My mother had a pair of brown leather shoes she had bought when a young woman. They were sleek, elegant and classy, timeless, made of soft Italian leather, stamped "Made in Italy" on the sole. Even after all this time, they are ageless. She kept them from the day she bought them until the day she died, even though she wasn't able to wear them for decades. Older feet and bad knees precluded her from sporting these special shoes.

I keep these shoes in memory of her, in memory of a happier person than she was at her death, a memory of a happier person than the woman I knew. They represented something for her and so for me, too. I never knew the woman who bought those shoes. It was before her debacle of a marriage, before children. I do not think that young woman lived the life that she expected to live.

My mother told me stories about her young self.

"I got fired from a job for wearing red shoes to work," she told me proudly, with a little bit of a giggle. I also had a pair of red shoes, but she called me a floozy.

"One night," she said, "I had two dates. I left the first one at the bus stop, ran home where the second one picked me up in his car. I ducked down as we passed the bus stop so the first date wouldn't see me."

This woman left her home in England, by herself, and moved to Italy to teach a wealthy family's children to speak English. When she left that job, she stayed in Naples and got a job at the NATO office there. She never went to college because there was only enough money for one to attend and her brother, as was the custom in those days, was the chosen one. Even so, she took the test to become a foreign correspondent and placed just below the score where she would have been accepted. I would have liked that woman. She had spirit, a sense of adventure.

There were glimpses of that confidant woman a couple of times in my life. When I was about 14 or 15 she went to New York City and found a job. She was ecstatic. She loved being in the city. But my father made it so miserable at home for her that she quit. Later in her life, after her divorce and her children were grown, after my brother had moved to Prague in the Czech Republic, she took a course in teaching English as a second language. She went to Prague and lived there for six months as a teacher; she was in her 70's at the time.

At her funeral, a close friend of hers gave the eulogy and spoke about how my mother had enlightened her about Thoreau and how he had written about the beaches on Cape

Cod where they were then standing. I did not know the woman her friend described.

I wish I had known the woman who wore those shoes. I only knew the one who wanted to "save" me. She wanted to protect me from hurt and pain, from my "impulsiveness" that she herself had once lived out as a young woman, and from all the resulting failures. But really, what kind of life is that? Scared to try anything new, to take any risks? She tried to mold me into the woman she wished she was. What she taught me was not to like myself, not to believe in myself.

When I was in my twenties I liked black boots with tiny heels and pointy toes, click clacking on the sidewalk. That was the time I was supposed to be figuring out who I wanted to be. I never would have worn those brown shoes; they're not who I am. I spent most of my life trying to fulfill her dreams, even if they weren't mine.

These shoes are a reminder that once she was happy. I did not know her as a happy woman. I wish I had. What adventures we would have had.

DARK DAYS

I know the forewarnings of the darkness to come. The anxiety. A constrictor tightening around my throat until I can't breathe. Any demand, sound or touch will drive me mad. I slowly back into my burrow and close the opening with rocks so I can be alone in quiet stillness, create a solid wall of silence around me.

But I know the black serpents are there. I see their bodies slithering towards me. Striking fast, poison destroying my intentions, plunging me into an unconscious abyss. I am worthless, a no-talent whiner.

"Why even try?" they hiss until I am paralyzed by their venom.

Eyes pleading, as I die a slow death. *This is too hard to fight for my life* is my overriding thought on days like this. It would be so easy to take the knife and let the poison and my blood gush out of my body.

Sometimes I try to find my way out of this dark jungle, but it never works. I trip, tumbling, scraped and bruised.

"It's only chemicals," I tell myself.

Chemicals mixing and churning in my brain to create a recipe for chaos. That relieves the pain some. If I just sit beneath a tree, screened from the rain, I will be able to breathe again.

O To Be A Dragon

"my wish...O to be a dragon"
— "O to Be a Dragon" by Marianne Moore

It comes out of nowhere, this inescapable anxiety. But if I were a dragon...I'd feel the beat of my powerful wings as I take to the air, soaring in the sky. My thoughts would no longer race around in my head so fast I can't grab onto any one of them. I would have space to spread my arms, push the crowds of people away. It would give me the silence I need to slow my brain, the quiet to calm my quivering body.

I need to banish the voices in my head. The ones that judge every single thing I do. The ones that tell me I don't know what is best for me. The ones that tell me everything I do and think is flawed. I am afraid to make the wrong move, the wrong choice. I never knew I could be who I wanted to be. I was *told* how to live, not *taught* how to live. I want to run, crying, yelling, shrieking, "LEAVE ME ALONE!" But, O to be a dragon.

A giant, benevolent monster. I am hurtling through the air, filled with sheer joy. The freedom, the solitude, the silence save for the whoosh of the wind in my ears as I glide and climb higher and higher. I am a behemoth, with scales for armor. I am not defenseless, vulnerable to harsh words: bastard, bitch, impulsive, lazy. I am feared. I am invincible.

O to be a dragon.

FORGIVENESS

I think I forgive her, my mother.
        Oblivious to my beaten down soul
             I was her emotional punching bag
                To relieve her frustration
                For the life she did not want,
                For the life she had hoped to live,
                    unfulfilled

Denied
      true mother love.
            The love that permits her child to sail
                into a world of her own discovery,
                even when the child's compass malfunctions.

Dismissed and ignored
      if I skipped down my yellow brick road
      she herded me back to her track
          with a switch to the back

Questioned
      Bright light in my eyes,
      I was treated as if I were a murderer
      of the one she loved the most,
          herself.

My essence
      had to be annihilated
      to save her from the same fate.
      So that I could live *her* dreams

My mother
      was not capable of embracing my differences.
      And time without her has given me peace.

I think I forgive her, my mother
      for she knew not what she did.

SILENCE

Silence when generated by someone else can be twisted into tension or crafted into peace. Fashioned by yourself, it soothes; it creates silence within the mind. Silence is a blessing for me but also a curse. Years of silence used as a weapon has left me scarred. Years when I created my own silence have given me peace.

Silence can be deafening. It can put me on edge. This silence is filled with unspoken words. A silence forced upon me. Even if I did offend you unknowingly, still, is this what I deserve? It fills me with anxiety over the unknowns. It is a rejection, a boundary drawn between me and you, the silencer. It festers into a blister that finally pops in an emotional bomb. I can hear the tick tick tick before it explodes. My only chance of diffusing it is to speak.

Silence created by anger establishes distance. It softens the intense emotions so that reason can emerge. I know shouting will not unscramble the mess. Resolution is realized when I know my emotional needs—and that they have not been satisfied. It is realized when I understand that it is acceptable for me to crave compassion and validation for myself.

When the voices in my head can finally be quashed and I am able to savor my thoughts, that is a silence I cherish. I can follow a thread of an idea wherever it may lead. Soft sounds like wind blowing through the trees, the flutter of birds' wings as they fly overhead, soaring into the tranquility of the sky. These are sounds in silence that do not overwhelm my ears, jarring me into a fight or flight state of mind.

And who hasn't felt the grief of the silence when you want to talk to someone you know is no longer, whom you'll never speak to again? This is a silence that makes your heart ache; tears stream down your face as you experience the truth of a loved one's passing. It comes on you suddenly and unexpectedly, even years after you've said goodbye.

She was still my mother and sometimes I miss her.

RESOLUTION

Acceptance brings its own kind of silence. A truce within yourself. An agreement that all that can be said has been told, discussed, shouted, screamed. You've decided to move on and leave behind the bitterness. The pardoned does not have to have regrets, does not even need to know they are absolved. The silence of acceptance is for the victim. It liberates the pardoner from the burden of resentment.

My mother was lying in a hospital bed at this pivotal moment for me. She was coming to the end of her life. I think somewhere deep down she knew she had failed me, but her narcissism demanded that she justify her actions. I was sitting in her hospital room, chatting, when she said to me, "You wouldn't be so creative if it wasn't for me. And you wouldn't be as avid a reader if I hadn't taught you how to read."

It finally hit me: twenty years of therapy had not gotten through to me completely like those two statements. I thought, "This woman doesn't see me as anything but an extension of her. I'm not a separate person in her mind!"

A light switch went on, click. Maybe because I had spent so much time untangling myself from her, creating a life that I wanted to live, I wasn't able to understand this before that moment.

I was furious at first. How can someone truly believe that another person would not be anything without their input? That wasn't nurturing; it was molding.

I thought about how I had worked to disentangle myself from her, to break the net that had enmeshed me, to escape.

"What is the point," I asked myself, "in being angry with someone who will never understand, who is incapable of understanding my frustration and fury?"

Everyone has a choice. You can carry animosity with you throughout your life. It creates a distrust of everyone, a cynicism that invades your every day. Resentment is a crutch so that you do not have to take any risks. It isolates you in the idea that you are protecting yourself from hurt and betrayal. It delivers unsatisfied dreams. It robs you of contentment.

Acceptance is not weakness. It does not mean I have given up my soul. I will not wait until the offender apologizes.

I choose acceptance.

ROYALINE B. EDWARDS

Author's Note: Kandi's story began in 1943, when, at age 7, her family made a life-changing move from their small southern town, Granville, Georgia, to a large industrial city, Columbus, Ohio. Her excitement bordered the mixed emotions of her parents, James and Fannie Kane, her fourteen-year old sister, Elsie, nine-year old brother, Rickey, and three-year old brother, Ray-Jay.

The long two day train ride was worth it, Kandi's parents had reasoned. It was time to leave that insufferable system of segregation for a new life with new opportunities for them and their children.

Kandi's and her family's adjustment to their new life up north was made easier with help from Uncle Ben and Aunt Sadie, Fannie's sister. School was a turning point for Kandi, both personal and socially, as she grappled with a close-up view of integration and new-found freedoms, such as being able to use the public library, ride on a bus and sit wherever there was an empty sit, or the extra help in school for a speech impediment that often sent her to her refuge, her love of art, when she needed to express herself. The run-in with a school yard bully proved to be another building block that shaped and reshaped her personality.

Flashback stories of her mother's growing-up days revealed an inner strength that Kandi leaned on after entering middle school: a heart-wrenching experience of one of her close friends that left a deep wound that would set Kandi back temporarily.

Upon entering high school, Kandi learned more of the details of her Mother's brother, who went missing in Georgia years before. It was the results of this knowledge that Kandi would, with determination and resolve, stretch her wings to find out what actually happened to her Uncle Tripe.

Kandi's college days were marked with successes and failures in her attempt to enter law school.

Acknowledgments are in order to my very patient husband, Kelvin, for his love and patience in keeping me focused on my destination with Kandi, and the hours spent in leading me to the next level in using the computer more effectively; to my friend Linda Hillier, a fellow student I first met in the class *Writing for Children and Young Adults*, who offered me candid remarks coupled with her excitement about Kandi's future; and to Bob, the instructor of that class whose style of teaching proved to be an excellent fit for me.

Kandi

A New Beginning

The air was filled with excitement. I stood in awe of the shiny, black engine puffing billows of black and white smoke, smoke that formed odd funny shapes that floated and blended into the blue sky. My imagination was on the loose. Suddenly, a booming voice rang out, "All Aboard!"

"Kandi!' my mother said, tightening her grip on my hand. Her other hand gripped the large colorful bag we all knew as her *survival* bag. "Hurry, it's time to board the train."

The long platform looked like it had no end. Ahead, I saw Daddy trying to balance Ray-Jay, my three-year old brother, in one arm, while he carried an old tattered suitcase—tied with extra rope. A man wearing a red cap walked close behind Daddy pulling a wagon piled high with our trunk, suitcases, and two of Mama's hat boxes teetering on top. Daddy told me later the man was a *Red Cap*. My 14 year old sister, Elsie, was holding tightly to my nine-year old brother Rickey with one hand, and in the other, the big shoebox filled with food for the long trip to Ohio.

Earlier that morning, Mama had fried chicken, baked biscuits, sliced the pound cake she had baked the day before, and made peanut butter sandwiches. We were the Kane family on our way to Columbus, Ohio from Granville, Georgia. It was June 1, 1943. I was seven years old.

By the time we got to the *Colored* section of the train, my feet were hurting in my new, black patent leather shoes. They were my first store-bought shoes; the little pinch I felt when I tried them on went away when I squeezed my toes a bit. I couldn't bear to leave those pretty shoes in the store.

"All Aboard!" shouted the booming voice again. Only this time, it was right in front of me. Seeing first his shiny black shoes, I slowly looked up to the giant looming over me. I blinked at the bright gold buttons that stood out against his black suit and black hat. He waved us on board. Scared and excited at the same time, I stared at the long aisle of seats on both sides. Passengers were twisting, smiling, and waving to people outside their windows.

Daddy boarded the train, and the man wearing the red cap helped him fit our other suitcases in the rack above the double seats he had saved for us. Ray-Jay was like a jumping bean, popping up and down from seat to seat. I wanted to sit next to the large window, but Elsie and Rickey got there first, so I sat between Mama and Elsie, while Ray-Jay sat between Daddy and Rickey. Patting my hand gently, Mama whispered, "This is a long trip, you'll get a turn at the window."

Suddenly, the train jerked and started moving slowly, then stopped again. "What happened, Mama?" I asked, feeling nervous.

Daddy smiled and said, "Don't worry, Kandi, once the train starts to move and builds up steam, the outside world will rush by like a picture show." And sure enough it did.

I settled back in my seat imagining those big iron wheels speeding over the many miles of railroad tracks taking us far away from Georgia. After a while, Mama started humming a fast little tune. When I looked up at her, her eyes were closed, and her face kept changing—sometimes happy, sometimes sad. Then she started swaying her body from side to side to the beat of the song she was humming. I didn't want her to catch me staring, so I touched her arm gently. She stopped humming, opened her eyes slowly, then looked down at me and smiled.

"Mama," I asked, "What's the name of that song you were humming. It's pretty." She didn't answer at first, just smiled and looked at Ray-Jay curled into a little ball on Daddy's lap, and Rickey and Elsie on each other's shoulders. All were napping.

"Great Day! Great Day!" Mama said, turning to me. Her voice sounded a little strange, and her eyes were kind of watery. I was about to ask her what was the matter when she said, "That's the name of the song. It's a spiritual our ancestors sang long ago. And it is a great day, Kandi, even though I am feeling both sad and happy."

"I don't understand," I said. "How can you mix happy and sad together? Is it like mixing sugar and salt?" wondering if they would taste good or yucky together.

Mama said, "It's hard to compare things outside the body with feelings that are inside the body. Happy and sad are feeling words, and there are times when the two become entangled or mixed up with each other—like when you want to laugh and cry at the same time. We grownups call it mixed emotions." Mama stopped talking and hugged me close.

"It is a great day, Kandi, because our family is leaving the south, a place that chipped away a part of me every time I would see the "White Only" signs in the windows of public restaurants, or public buildings, like the library, waiting rooms at train and bus stations, or benches in public parks or other public places—all of which we are taxed to help maintain, but can't use. Also, the outdated school textbooks often sent to our schools, while the newest editions go to the white schools first."

Pausing, Mama said softly, "I am also sad because we're leaving your Grandpa and Granny, aunties, uncles, cousins and friends. Saddest of all, I'll miss my birthplace, Georgia: its chalky red clay, Stone Mountain, clear running brooks and streams, draping Magnolia and Weeping Willow trees—all God's creations for all living beings to respect and enjoy."

Mama's talk made me think of the times when I would overhear grownups talk about somebody called Jim Crow, and what a sin and a shame how he wanted to keep Black people *in their place.*

I looked at Mama and asked, "Is sin about not liking people because they look different?"

Mama said, "That's a tough question to answer right now, Kandi. Let's put it on the shelf until later."

"But Mama," I said, feeling sadness in my chest, "why don't white people like us?" Did we do something bad to them?"

Mama's face made those changes again. Then she said softly, "Not all white people hate or dislike Black people because of our color. The same is true of Black people in their feelings about white people. We must remember..."

Ray-Jay's *um hungry song* interrupted our talk. It was time to eat. Soon, people were taking down and opening shoeboxes, fat brown grocery bags, and croaker sacks. One family had a big picnic basket.

Daddy laughed and said to Mama, "It won't be long before this car smells like Aunt Susie's kitchen..."

"Like when she's frying up a batch of chicken for the church supper," Mama said smiling, and giving me the look that our talk was on the shelf.

Soon the sky grew dark. Out came tiny, twinkling stars

popping out like far-away firecrackers; we all settled in our seats for sleeping the best we could. I tried, but my wide-awake eyes, dilly-dallying with my mind, made it flip flop from one image to another until I was back in Georgia overhearing Daddy say to Mama, "It's time to tell the kids, Fannie."

Mama had sighed and said, "Yes, James, I know, but I wish we didn't have to go. Papa and Granny are getting up in age, and I just hate moving so far away."

"I do, too", Daddy said, "But I got another letter from Ben that his boss still wants to hire me. You know I would never get such a job down here." That's how I found out we were moving up north, and it had made me sad.

The train's whistle jolted me back to the present, and somewhere between the jolt and the clickety clack of those big wheels taking us farther away from Georgia, I fell fast asleep.

The next morning, my wake-up call was the warm sun beaming down on my face. Mama and Daddy were busy gathering our belongings, while Rickey and Ray-Jay were yawning and stretching from the uncomfortable ride through the night. People rushed about getting their things and heading for the door. Pulling down our last suitcase, Daddy said, "Wait here while I go look for a *Red Cap*." I plopped down near a window because my feet were beginning to hurt.

"Look!" shouted Rickey. Ray-Jay ran to the window, stepping on my foot.

"Mama, Mama," Ray-Jay howled, "Train on fire!" On a nearby track was a train swooshing puffs of white and gray smoke from below.

"Oh, Ray-Jay," Mama said, hugging him, "that's just the train letting off steam. In a few minutes, we'll be in the waiting room." Satisfied there was no fire, Ray-Jay began his *Um hungry song.*

Daddy returned with a *Red Cap*, and, with his help, we made it off the train. I looked down at my pretty black patent leather shoes, and with every step, wished I could kick them off, freeing my crowded toes.

Once inside, I hobbled as fast as I could to a row of empty

seats and tried slipping my feet free, but they would not budge.

"What's the matter?" Mama asked, taking something from her survival bag. Daddy, seeing my tears, sat next to me and wiggled my feet free. He then hurried to one of the ticket windows for information about our next train. Mama looked at me, smiled and handed me my old shoes.

"Mama, you didn't throw them away!" Everybody watched as I slipped my feet easily into my old, throw-away shoes and pranced around like a princess. I looked up to see Daddy rushing toward us, and he didn't look happy.

"Okay," he said, "our train is on track twelve, and we need to board now!"

It wasn't long before the *Red Cap*, with our suitcases piled high on his wagon, was zigzagging through the crowd, far ahead of us. All of us knew where we needed to be with each other. With so many people rushing about, it was hard keeping the *Red Cap* in sight. We finally boarded the Baltimore & Ohio train that would take us to our new home.

I nearly tripped over Mama's big survival bag, rushing to get the window seat. Rickey pouted, but Mama reminded him that he'd had his turn. I glued my face to the big, wide window, in wonder of the picture frames that moved quickly by.

"Mama! Daddy! Look at all the pretty houses and barns," I said loudly. I thought of asking Mama for my pad and pencil, but I didn't want to miss anything!

Morning tiptoed into the quiet afternoon. Somewhere in between, I fell asleep. When I woke up and looked around, I tugged Mama's sleeve, pointing to the new people sitting in the seats across from us. I whispered, "Mama, look!"

Mama smiled and said quietly, "This train is headed north, and we are now over the Mason Dixon Line, so we can sit anywhere we like."

"Where is the line? Can I see it? Is it painted on the roads?" I asked, wondering how big and long it was. Mama was about to explain when we heard the booming voice of the conductor, "Next stop, Columbus!"

MIXED EMOTIONS

Uncle Ben met us at the train station and, after several attempts to fit our belongings into and on top of his old, cranky station wagon, we were finally on our way. Daddy said later that Ray-Jay, Rickey, and I fell asleep like dominoes.

"We're here," Mama said, gently shaking us awake. It took almost as much time getting out of Uncle Ben's station wagon as it did getting from the train station!

Everything looked and felt strange to me. What funny-looking houses, I thought to myself. "Uncle Ben," I said, "why are the houses stuck together?"

Uncle Ben laughed and said, "These are row houses, kids."

"Why are there are so many of them?" I asked, shifting from one foot to the other in my comfortable old shoes. "Which one do you live in?" A door opened and there stood Aunt Sadie, Mama's oldest sister.

"Lordy, me!" she said. "Here you are. Come on in. I got food waiting 'cause I know some little tummies are growling aplenty." Once we were inside, she locked the screen door. Then, spreading her big, long arms wide, she gathered us kids into them—giving us tight hugs and kisses on our forehead. Letting go, she said, "Stand back and let me look at you young'uns." Ray-Jay and Rickey stared at Aunt Sadie, with side glances at all the fixings on the table. Soon our tummies were happy, and Aunt Sadie led us upstairs to the space our family would share until we could find a place of our own.

After two weeks of house hunting, Daddy and Uncle Ben found a rent house about four blocks away. It was a five-room, shotgun duplex that we all had a hard time fitting into. But, we were happy until those pests showed up. Mama soon declared war on those critters, and before long every possible place for them to gnaw their way in was plugged with tin can tops, and we kids were given strict orders to leave no food around to get them liking us.

SETTLING IN

Our small backyard had a fence that separated us from an old two-story barn. It had a long path that led to a big brown house. I liked the old barn, with its shiny red paint, and two big doors held together with a big black latch. I wasn't sure about the open hayloft; it made me a little nervous.

One day, Rickey and I were playing near the fence. With a grin on his face, he pointed to the hayloft. "Kandi," he said slyly. "I betcha you can't jump from that hayloft."

Seeing Mamma at the window, I said, "I betcha you're about to be in big trouble."

Mama rushed out, caught our attention and whispered, "Kandi, you and Rickey stay away from that fence! White folks live there, and we don't want trouble." I wondered why Mama was whispering—no one else was around. Besides, I knew who lived there. It was a girl about my age. Her hair was red; she had been playing near the brown house the day we moved in.

Mama was right about changes we would have to get used to, and it seemed new ones popped up every day. September brought a big one.

It was day three and Ray-Jay stood in the middle of the floor screaming, "I don't wanna go!" He didn't like being dropped off at Aunt Sadie's for the day ever since Mama had found a job. Suddenly, he stopped screaming. You could hear a pin drop. At the door was Mama with *The Look*; it meant the end of the hugs and cuddling Ray-Jay had settled for. For the rest of the week, his screaming turned into a little whine that we could all live with.

Finally, we all knew where we were supposed to be for the day, starting with Daddy leaving for work before the break of day. Now, the strangest feeling for me was the first day of school—none of my teachers had brown skin! Before leaving Georgia, we were told how different our lives would be in a big city up north. I could not believe my eyes when the teacher gave us school supplies, along with new books! We even had different teachers for art, gym and music. In Georgia, our small elementary school had one teacher for each grade up to fifth grade. They taught everything!

At recess time, my joy faded when I saw the big playground with swings, see-saws, something called monkey bars and spaces to play hopscotch. I searched for Rickey's face, but he was nowhere to be seen. I learned later there were two playgrounds— one for boys and one for girls. Back home, we all played together.

I was feeling sad and alone, until a gentle hand rested on my shoulders. With relief, I looked up into the smiling face of my teacher, Miz Dalton. Standing next to her was a girl with a friendly smile. Miz Dalton said, "This is Sarah, our classroom helper this week. She will show you around the playground and where to line up when the bell rings."

Sarah took my hand and said, "Let's race to the swing set." She let go of my hand. "Come on Kandi, there's only one swing left!" Sarah was a talker, but being shy, I didn't mind at all. I liked the sounds of her words. Next, we raced to the teeter-totter and were about to jump on when a girl with red hair came over. "Hi Penny," said Sarah. "Want to play with us?"

Penny and I stared at each other. Feeling nervous, I said hi, but she didn't say hi back. Instead, she ran and jumped on the teeter-totter. I watched as she and Sarah bobbed up and down laughing and talking so fast I could hardly keep up with what they were saying. I guess my ears will have to learn to listen faster I laughed to myself.

When they got off, Penny looked at me and asked, "What's your name?"

"Kandi," I said in my slow, southern drawl. She giggled. After that, my tongue glued itself to the roof of my mouth for the rest of recess. That evening, I drew pictures of my first day at school.

NEIGHBORLY ENCOUNTERS

One Saturday, when Rickey and I were playing near the fence Mama had warned us about, a boy and girl came out of the big brown house and started running down the path toward the barn. When they saw us, they stopped and stared. We stared back. I turned to leave, but stopped. It was the girl's red hair—it *was* Penny!

"Hi Kandi," she said moving closer to the fence. She remembered my name, I thought.

Looking at Rickey, the boy asked, "What's your name?"

"Rickey."

"I'm Seth. Wanna play?" he asked.

"Play what?' Rickey answered, eyeing me and slowly moving away from the fence.

"Hide and Seek," he said.

"Where?" asked Rickey.

"There," he said, pointing to the barn.

Grinning, Penny whispered to me, "I know places to hide where they will never find us, especially in the loft."

I wanted to say I didn't want to play in that scary loft, but the words got stuck on my tongue.

"I don't know," Rickey said slowly. "My Mama told us to stay on this side of the fence 'cause we don't want trouble."

I was waiting for Penny and Seth to giggle at Rickey's southern talk. They didn't, but before we could decide on the hide-and-seek thing, Mama came to the door, gave us *The Look* and said it was time to eat. While we didn't play that day, we would in days to come—we became friends.

It was Saturday, and the *thu-bump, thu-bump* of our second-hand Maytag washer meant it was wash day.

I got up, peeked out the window, and watched the clothes on the clothesline swaying in the breeze. In my head, I put heads and limbs on some of the clothes and was about to get my drawing pad when, from outside, I heard an unfamiliar voice.

"I guess you might say we're 'backyard' neighbors. I'm Mary Anderson, Seth and Penny's mom.

"Nice to meet you, Mrs. Anderson," Mama said slowly.

"Oh, please, call me Mary," she answered.

Stumbling a bit, Mama said, "I-I'm Fannie Kane."

"Well, it's nice to meet you, too, Fannie. Seth and Penny are always talking about Rickey and Kandi. Moving closer to the fence, she said, "Today, I baked cookies for Seth's Boy Scout Troop and after putting the last batch in the oven, I saw you at the clothesline, and thought I would welcome you to the neighborhood with these." She handed a covered dish to Mama.

"Why, that's mighty nice of you to do that, Miss, uh...Mary," Mama said smiling and looking surprised at the same time. Once those cookies were on our kitchen table, they flew off that plate like they had wings!

SNOW DRIFTS

Time passed quickly. One morning, I woke up to the most beautiful sight. Outside, everything was shiny white! Rooftops were piled high with soft, white snow, while tree limbs bowed gently under the burden of it. This was my first time seeing so much snow, and I could hardly wait to get out in it—and I did.

"Kandi!" Mama shouted, standing at the door shaking. "Don't you know you can't play outside dressed that way? This is not Georgia!"

"It's fun, Mama." Gathering handfuls, I threw the snow up, letting it fall around me. A few days later, I was tucked snuggly under heavy quilts, with cod liver oil, Vicks Salve and taking some really yucky, nasty-tasting stuff in a brown bottle called *Father John*.

Mama tried to convince me it would help shoo my cold away, but I wasn't sure about that at all!

That winter seemed a hop, skip, and a jump and it soon gave over to spring and the news that our dream would come true. Uncle Ben found a bigger house for rent on Parker Street. We were all very excited. I didn't say much because I felt a little sad thinking about leaving my new friends and the old barn, now a favorite place to play.

When we saw the size of the house, there was much oohing and aahing, squirming and giggling and wondering why it was taking so long for Uncle Ben to park the car. Once inside, we all claimed our own little territory, especially the large fenced-in backyard. Later, as we were getting into Uncle Ben's car for home, I looked up to see a man's face disappear from the upstairs window of the house next door.

A few weeks later, the new house "bubble" popped liked a balloon, shattering dreams of happiness for our family. We were told the neighbor next door complained he didn't want a bunch of noisy kids living next door to him. Sometime later, we found out the real reason, when Uncle Ben came over to return Daddy's deposit money.

"I'm sorry things didn't work out about the house," Uncle Ben said. "But you know how it is in this country."

"Yeah, I know," said Daddy in voice that sounded more sad than angry. "I thought it might be different up here, but not much. It's just not as full in your face as down south." Uncle Ben walked over, patted Daddy on the shoulder and left.

Everybody found something to do after saying good-bye to Uncle Ben. Mama started dinner, Rickey took Ray-Jay for a ride in his new wagon, and Elsie turned on the radio to listen to *The Shadow*.

Daddy was slumped down on the davenport, his head resting on the back and his eyes closed when I came back with my pad and pencil. I just wanted to do something so his sad and happy feelings wouldn't get all mixed up like Mama's. It was hard for me to understand that the reason we didn't get the house was more about the color of our skin than anything else: we were just normal people showing happiness and excitement about having a bigger and nicer place to live. I hoped my pictures would cheer Daddy up.

The next day was a rainy Saturday. The smell of bacon meant Mama was making our favorite breakfast, after getting Daddy off to work at his part-time job.

Mama said, "We were all disappointed about yesterday, but I don't want you kids to feel you did something wrong. Well, I have another story to tell you about your Uncle Tripe."

Rickey and I asked, "Does he get into more trouble?"

"Wait and see," said Mama. She pulled up the usual high stool she used when reading or telling us stories.

"Mama," said Elsie, "Since I already know most of Uncle Tripe's childhood adventures, I'll take Ray-Jay to visit Aunt Sadie." Mama was a good storyteller, and we didn't mind, especially since it was a rainy day.

At first, she didn't say anything—just looked at us with a smile. Then she brought her hands together, locking her fingers, then slowly opened them as the signal to begin a once-upon-a-time story. "Now, she said, "Let's travel back for a short family history lesson.

Mama's Story

A long time ago, when my grandparents, Samuel Smith and Viola Simmons, *jumped the broom*, meaning got married, they had a large family—six sons and four daughters. They lived in a big farm house that sat on 24 acres of land, and whenever a son *jumped the broom*, he and his bride were given a piece of it once a new Smith baby was on the way. John, my daddy, was their fifth child. *He jumped the broom* with my Mama, Sally Blanton, and it wasn't long before there were three of us: Sadie, Tripe, and myself.

Our land was a long walk to Paw-Paw and Granny V's farm house, but Tripe and I didn't mind, especially if it was a warm, sunny day and Mama said we could go. One day, we were about half way there when Tripe shouted, "Look, Fannie!" Turning in the direction he was pointing, I was surprised to see a little brook that led to a clump of small trees.

"Come on, Fannie," he said, his eyes bright with mischief, as whenever he wanted to do something he shouldn't. "We're not too far from Paw-Paw and Granny Vee's. It could be a short cut, with some juicy blackberries along the way." Not really wanting to, I left the path and followed Tripe until we got to the trees.

"I don't think I want to go in there," I said, standing back. Tripe grabbed my hand and pulled me along.

"Don't be so scared, Fannie. I'll protect you."

We followed the little brook until we got to a big open space. There was a small lake with water so clear you could see your face in it.

"Sure wish I could swim," Tripe said, inching closer to the bank.

"Come on, Tripe, Let's go."

"I watched cousins Jonathan and Thomas at the old mill pond last week, and swimming looked kinda easy. Wanna try it?"

"No!" I said, now getting scared. "There could be a monster down there." Pulling Tripe by the arm, I said, "Let's go back home." At the mention of a monster, Tripe backed away. "We can tell Mama we changed our minds about going to Paw-Paw and Granny Vee's."

Turning to leave, we heard a big swooshing sound that made us look back to see a huge stream of water spouting from the middle of the lake. Feeling wetness from the spray of the water, I started running and screaming, "Come on, Tripe!"

I didn't know Tripe could run so fast. He whizzed by me like Flash Gordon, and was on the path heading home by the time I was half there. So much for protecting me, I thought, trying to catch up with him.

Leaving out the swimming part, we told Daddy and Mama about our little adventure at the supper table.

In a stern voice, Daddy said, "That lake is not a place for you two. It's pretty, but dangerous. You can't swim, and there are water moccasins aplenty, and Lord knows what else. It's time you two have more chores to do."

Missing Daddy's warning tone, Tripe said, "We can learn to swim, and I'm not afraid of snakes."

"You speak for yourself, Tripe," I said, giving him the eye about the part of the story we left out. From that day on, I was happy to help my older sister Sadie gather the eggs from the henhouse, learn how to churn butter, and later how to knit and sew.

Each passing year brought its special ups and downs to large and small country families. We planted and harvested vegetable gardens, fruit orchards, sewed most of our own clothes—often passed down through several generations. Younger kids watched while old siblings designed and completed scooters and wagons from worn-out wheels, discarded crates, and unearthed artifacts from the nearby junkyard. Others found joy in fishing and hunting. In late fall, every six to sixteen year-old Smith trudged to the one-room schoolhouse for the 3 R's, based on Granny Vee's conviction that once we had them inside our heads, we would be on the road to freedom.

Sunday, considered our rest day, was way out of step to our way of thinking, because we had to go to Little Zion Baptist Church to listen to Rev. Joshua Johnson.

His preaching, slow and deliberate, often began with "Brothers and sisters, we have to keep the faith and love everybody if we want a place in heaven."

About an hour later, his heavy voice would increase in volume and tempo, jolting awake all nappers and snoozers like us kids.

"We're tired of being under bondage like the children of Israel! How much longer do we have to wait to enjoy the freedom to get good jobs and live wherever we wish? How much longer do we have to wait before we are free to go to the polls and vote without fear for our lives? We are all human beings, with God-given rights, before we are anything else."
Those words meant he was on his way to what we kids called Whoopsville.

Most of the grown-ups began answering back with loud voices of, "Amen! Amen!" Sister Nellie Johnson would whip out her *Gospel Pearl* song book, followed by others, and before long, shouts and singing filled the church.

Sister Cordelia Walker, seeing those *Gospel Pearl* books, would make her way to the old, tired, worn-out, hand-me-down piano. She would slowly touch a few keys, and suddenly those tired, cotton-picking fingers would fly over them like birds flying over a cornfield. At last, we kids were free to move our bodies from side to side, clap our hands and tap our feet to the music.

The service ended when Deacon Dan Beaver, in his closing prayer, reminded everyone to send up their timbers to the Lord each day and have faith that life would soon get better for us all. That faith would be put to the test years later.

Time brought tears of joy at new births and tears of sorrows at deaths. In 1913, we gathered to say farewell to Paw-Paw and Granny Vee. They passed away within three days of each other. Paw-Paw succumbed to pneumonia, Granny Vee of a broken heart.

Feeling Mama was near the end of her story, I said, "Mama, I think I know now how sadness and happiness can get mixed up. It's like when we are born, there is happiness, but underneath is sadness because the newborn will grow up like us, wondering how long it will take to be truly free in our country."

LINDA CONTI

Author's Note: (for adult readers): Our world is incredibly diverse in many, many ways: the people who live in it; the natural environment—the trees, oceans, lakes, mountains and more; the fascinating wildlife—deer, raccoons, fox and coyotes; and the many, many wonderful birds who grace our daily lives with their amazing flight, beautiful colors and sweet songs.

These wonderful birds remind us of nature's incredible gifts. It is my hope that this series of books, "A Bird's Life...", will give children a glimpse into the extraordinary lives of some of these birds and foster a great love and respect for them. Please share your appreciation of these marvelous creatures and help protect our wildlife!

For my great-niece, Abigail, and young friend, Olee.

Sweetie Pie and the Other Colorful Birds in Mrs. Bumberly's Backyard

MRS. BUMBERLY LIVES IN A SMALL YELLOW HOUSE with a big backyard and a nice, grassy lawn.

Her yard has two blueberry bushes, one small cherry tree—which she planted just last year—and tall, tall pine trees reaching SO HIGH into the sky that Mrs. Bumberly has to Stretch, Stretch, Stretch her neck just to see the tips of them!

Mrs. Bumberly loves the many colorful birds who come to visit.

In winter, when cold settles in and the berries are all gone from the bushes, Mrs. Bumberly likes to put food out for the birds. So that even in the coldest part of winter, when snow topples the trees and brisk winds blow, the birds still have enough have food to eat.

Today is Saturday, a fine warm, breezy day in early April. Wisps of white clouds dance through a blue, blue sky. In New Hampshire, where Mrs. Bumberly lives, the snow that blanketed her big backyard just last week has all melted. The brown grass of winter soon will turn a bright, happy green!

Mrs. Bumberly is in her kitchen, having just finished washing the breakfast dishes, when she happens to look out her window to her big backyard. Suddenly she sees a small flash of blue dash through the sky then land, WHOOSH, right on a tree branch.

"Oh, oh, oh," she exclaims, "I think it's a bluebird!" Mrs. Bumberly has never seen a bluebird in her backyard before!

"Just look at those beautiful blue and rosy-brown feathers." And, very slowly, Mrs. Bumberly opens her kitchen window, just a tiny bit, to get a better look. It was then that she hears the little bird singing!

"TUH-TOO-DUH-WEE, TUH-TOO-DUH-WEE" sings the little bluebird in a soft, sweet voice. "Spring is on the way. My friends from the south soon will come to play. Up to the sky—high—we'll fly, then dart to the ground—low—we'll go, stretching our feathers all the way out, gazing and swooping so happy about! TUH-TOO-DUH-WEE, TUH-TOO-DUH-WEE, TUH-TOO-DUH-WEE."

"Oh, how sweet! What a sweet song," exclaims Mrs. Bumberly. And right then and there, she decides to call the little bluebird, Sweetie Pie.

Wanting to get a better look at Sweetie Pie, Mrs. Bumberly heads outside to check her bird feeders.

So, she removes her pink-flowery apron, zips on her brown furry coat, picks up the big yellow bucket of bird food, and heads outside.

Of course, she doesn't want to frighten Sweetie Pie away, so she goes about filling the feeders, admiring Sweetie Pie as she goes.

Meanwhile, Sweetie Pie, still singing, moves to a branch where she can keep her eye on her favorite food. Suddenly, her branch takes an unexpected bounce! FLOOP! And another bluebird lands next to Sweetie Pie and starts chattering.

"What could those two bluebirds be chattering about," exclaims Mrs. Bumberly. At that same moment, she hears four-year-old Abigail from the yard next door shouting, "Hi, Mrs. Bumberly!"

"Abigail, hi! Come see the bluebirds!"

Abigail comes running over.

Abigail has been learning about birds in school and she loves birds as much as Mrs. Bumberly. She also loves helping Mrs. Bumberly fill the feeders and play a game of naming all the colorful birds that happen by.

"Abigail, look up there, see the two little birds with blue feathers. The one with the blue and rosy-brown feathers has been sitting outside my kitchen window all morning. That's Sweetie Pie."

"Hi birdies!" Abigail greets them. "Hi Sweetie Pie! What is the other bluebird's name?"

"Abigail, why don't you pick a name?"

So, Abigail fixes a thoughtful gaze on the bluebird next to Sweetie Pie. "Well, he's very, very blue!" she says. "I know, let's call him Blueberry!"

It was quite the most perfect name. Not only because of the color of Blueberry's blue feathers, but because blueberries are one of his favorite foods!

"My, how the two bluebirds are chattering! I wonder what they're saying, Abigail."

"Do birds really talk, Mrs. Bumberly?"

"Not like we do, but they can communicate with each other. I wonder what they're saying."

> "Hey, Sweetie Pie, what's up?" asks Blueberry.
>
> "I'm watching that lady and little girl looking at me." Sweetie Pie giggles, "Look how excited they are, ha ha!"
>
> "Ha, ha, I bet they've never

seen bluebirds before!"
laughs Blueberry.

"I thought I'd sing them a
song!" says Sweetie Pie, and
sings "TUH-TOO-DUH-
WEE, TUH-TOO-DUH-
WEE, TUH-TOO-DUH-
WEE, TOWEE-TOWEE-
TOWEE!"

"You're such a ham,
Sweetie Pie!" jokes
Blueberry, flapping his
wings for show. "I bet they
wish they could fly like us!"

Then PLOOP! The branch above Sweetie Pie and Blueberry
quivers and two dashing red cardinals come in for a landing.

It's Rudy, with very red feathers like Rudolph the reindeer's
bright red nose.

Next to Rudy is his friend, Shy Rosy, who has pale red
feathers and a very shy nature.

"Mmmmm, delicious!" Rudy
says, referring to a sunflower
nut he has just pecked from
a bird feeder. He puffs out
his red feathers, saying, "I've
been getting fat on these nuts
all winter long. But, it's been
so cold and windy, I need the
extra feathers! This winter
coat of mine keeps me warm,
but I'm glad spring will soon
be here, so I can shed some

of these feathers. Plus, I can't
wait for the blueberry bushes
to grow with those yummy,
juicy berries!"

"I love those blueberries,
too," chimes in Sweetie
Pie, remembering just how
sweet they taste. "Mmmmm,
blueberries and sunflower
nuts. Yum!"

"You're both plain nutty,"
teases Shy Rosy. "My favorite
food is crickets!"

While all this was going on, a few more colorful birds find
their way to Mrs. Bumberly's backyard.

Sweetie Pie sighs, "I wonder
if any food will be left over
for me?" but patiently stays
in the warm sunlight. Shy
Rosy flaps a wing at Rudy
and says, "It's the finches
again! Let's go see what
they're up to."

Blueberry flies off with Rudy and Shy Rosy while Sweetie Pie
continues to bask in the sun.

The finches also catch Abigail and Mrs. Bumberly's attention.
Abigail yells, "Oh boy, it's the Buttercups!"—her favorite name
for them.

How perky they are! Zooming in fast, WOWIE-ZOWIE,
landing on a bush or the spindly needle of an evergreen tree—
grabbing thistle from a feeder.

"Hey Finches," yells Rudy, "I
see you guys still have your dull
brown winter coats! Not long
now, Goldie, before you can
show off your bright yellow
feathers."

"Hey, don't give me a hard
time about my feathers!"
fires back Goldie, the little
goldfinch. "Rudy, you should
be so lucky! You only get new
feathers once a year! Soon I'll
have my brand new yellow
feathers and everyone will
admire my stunning plumage!
Isn't that right, Razzy?" Goldie
says, turning to the little
purple finch, who is busy
ruffling feathers that are more
raspberry-colored than purple.

Amused by all of this is Pepper, a tiny black-capped chickadee
who overhears their conversation while she has been searching
in a poplar tree for that tasty seed she hid in there last fall.

Suddenly, "Watch out,"
shouts Sweetie Pie. "Here
comes Bonkers, that noisy
blue jay!"

Bonkers has blue coloring, too, but is twice as big as Sweetie
Pie and twice as noisy!
He swoops down with a "Yeeek, Yeeek, Yeeek, Yeeek, Yeeek,"
then hops on the ground impatiently wanting some nuts.

In a panic, the finches quickly head for the bushes. Then one finch calls out, "Oh, it's ok, it's only noisy Bonkers coming to bother us again." Unfazed by Bonker's noise, the finches return to the feeders.

In the meantime, Woody, the red-bellied woodpecker, pokes his head out from where he was pecking at an old oak tree, TAP, TAP, TAPPING his long, sharp beak into the trunk, stuffing in bark and insects. Sometimes making a hole so big, a small bird could use it for a nest.

Woody flies to another tree and his distinct "wuk, wuk, wuk, wuk, wuk, wuk, wuk, wuk" catches Mrs. Bumberly and Abigail's attention and they play a game of who can spot him first. "I bet I can," says Abigail. And sure enough, she spots his red-orange head, checkerboard back, and snowy white chest. "I see him," she yells.

"Where? I don't see him."

"Over there. See his red head?"

"I see him now! Abigail, good work," praises Mrs. Bumberly.

Sweetie Pie looks on and chuckles at the two of them playing such a silly game.

Then Pixie, the enterprising Robin, shows up searching the lawn for a worm.

And Daffy, a nuthatch, with that upside-down way of traveling down a tree, darts to a feeder, grabs a nut, darts back, then shimmies up to his previous post.

Soon, all but Sweetie Pie fly off. Some to look for places to build their nests. Some to gather twigs and dried grass—their nests in progress. Some to warm the eggs already laid. Others to keep watch for dangers that might come along.

But for Sweetie Pie... "It's time for MY BREAKFAST now!" She flies to a feeder, then high into the sky.

Abigail and Mrs. Bumberly watch her go, saying, "Bye, Sweetie Pie. Come back again soon!"

Abigail helps Mrs. Bumberly put away the big yellow bucket, then goes home for a morning nap.

Mrs. Bumberly puts on her flowery apron to make chocolate-cherry cookies she'll share later with the neighbors. Sighing happily, she thinks, "What a wonderful morning it's been!"

And, every day now, the happy, little bluebird, Sweetie Pie, visits Mrs. Bumberly's backyard.

As spring rolls on, more colorful birds from the south fly in. Including the Baltimore Orioles, with their bright orange feathers, who love the oranges and grape jelly Abigail puts out... The itsy-bitsy hummingbirds who nip at the flowers... And the red-breasted Grosbeaks...

Some birds stay around all year, even as snow topples the trees, and deer wander through the yard, and brisk winds blow. Some fly south to warmer climates, to return north again in spring to build nests for their babies.

How amazing these birds all are, singing and chattering away, dancing about the grass, flying through the sky.

Do you remember their names?
Do you remember their colors?

Oh, what a wonderful place, is Mrs. Bumberly's backyard. With her two blueberry bushes, the little cherry tree, and the tall, tall pine trees that reach HIGH, HIGH, HIGH into the sky.

But most of all because of her friends, Abigail, Sweetie Pie, and all the colorful birds that visit each day!

Mrs. Bumberly loves these birds so much. And hopes you will, too!

So, remember—always look into the trees, or high in the sky, or on your grassy lawn—and listen for the songs, calls, and chattering of birds! For one day, a bluebird just like Sweetie Pie may come to visit you!

CAST OF CHARACTERS

Mrs. Bumberly lives in a little yellow house and loves wildlife and birds of all kinds. She likes to spend time with her friends and family, enjoys reading, music, and theater, and loves to bake chocolate-cherry cookies that she shares with Abigail and her neighbors down the street.

Abigail is five-years-old and also enjoys the birds just like Mrs. Bumberly. Every spring, Abigail helps her mother put in new vegetable and flower gardens in their backyard. She is especially fond of dancing at home and at school.

Sweetie Pie and **Blueberry** are Eastern Bluebirds. Sweetie Pie is the very first bluebird that ever came to visit Mrs. Bumberly in her backyard. She is a female bluebird, recognized because of her soft rosy and blue feathers and is a young bluebird, about one-and-a-half years old. Blueberry is a male bluebird, easy to identify because of his blue feathers that are much brighter than Sweetie Pie's. Like other bluebirds, Sweetie Pie and Blueberry prefer to live in open spaces around trees. They eat insects like crickets, grasshoppers, and spiders and enjoy fruit, too—especially berries. The mealworms that Mrs. Bumberly puts out for them in her bird feeders are among their favorite foods. Bluebirds like Sweetie Pie and Blueberry are often associated with happiness and love—known for their beautiful color, sweet nature and friendly disposition. They are always on the alert for harsh weather and animals such as raccoons, cats, and bears.

Rudy and **Shy Rosy** are Northern Cardinals. Rudy has very bright red feathers because he is a boy. Shy Rosy's feathers are a soft reddish-brown because she is a girl. Cardinals who live in New Hampshire where Mrs. Bumberly lives often stay there all winter long, rather than fly south. They can be seen hopping through low branches, even in the thickest snow of winter. Or you may see them perched on a branch high in a tree, singing their song in the early morning. They often are among the first birds you will see at the break of day and among the last birds you will see when the sun goes down. They mainly eat seeds and fruit, but also like beetles, flies, and moths, and other insects. Rudy and Shy Rosy are especially fond of the sunflower nuts that Mrs. Bumberly puts out.

The Buttercups are all finches. Some are House Finches, some American Goldfinch, some Purple Finches. **Goldie** is an American Goldfinch. His feathers in winter are an olive-brown color with black-feathered wings. In spring, he sheds the olive-brown feathers for bright yellow ones. **Razzy** is a Purple Finch, with raspberry-colored feathers, even in winter. Finches are all very small birds, about five inches long or less, with a wingspan of only about three inches. The color of their feathers varies from finch to finch, ranging from brown to gray, bright yellow to raspberry-colored. Boy finches are much brighter in color than the girls. They fly and flit across Mrs. Bumberly's backyard very fast, cheeping as they go. They like to fly as if they are following a wave instead of a straight line. A great number of them will all be flocking around Mrs. Bumberly's bird feeders that are stocked with sunflower nuts or thistle seed.

Pepper is a Black-Capped Chickadee. She has a black cap on her head, white-feathered cheeks, a black chin (bib), a buff-colored chest, and a soft gray back. Her beak is very tiny and her eyes are hardly noticeable because of the black cap on the top of her head. She likes to fly in to a feeder, grab a quick sunflower nut, then fly quickly back to a branch, unlike the finches who will stay perched at the feeders for a few minutes. Chickadees may live on a farm or in the city. They are short and round and barely weigh anything. They like to build their nests in an opening or hole in the rotten branch of a tree. It might be an opening they carve out themselves, or one left by a Downy

Woodpecker. They are curious, social birds, and have many calls to communicate different messages to other chickadees.

Bonkers is a Blue Jay, with blue, black and white feathers. He is a much larger bird than Sweetie Pie, Pepper, Goldie, and even Rudy. Blue Jays have long tails and noisy personalities, and are not shy at all about going after food, even at Mrs. Bumberly's feeders. Though their feathers look blue, they actually are a brownish black color. The blue color is the result of the type of feathers they have and the way the light affects their color. They have a distinctive call that can alert other Blue Jays to a hawk that might be nearby. They are fond of acorns.

Woody is a Red-Bellied Woodpecker. He is a little larger than a Blue Jay and has a bright reddish-orange cap on his head with a striking black and white-feathered back and a white chest. Instead of perching on a branch, he likes to skirt up the trunk of a tree with his head pointing to the sky and his tail pointing to the ground. The oldest known woodpecker was 12 years old. They are fun to watch fly from trunk to trunk. They are easy to identify with their vivid color, unusual way of clinging to a tree, and distinctive calls.

Pixie is an American Robin. Although Mrs. Bumberly sees her frequently in spring and summer, she never sees her in winter, so perhaps she flies to a warmer climate at that time of year. She is larger than a bluebird, almost as long as a Blue Jay, but much rounder than the Blue Jay. She has an orange-brownish chest, and a brown and grayish-black head and back. Her cheery song in the morning is a welcome sound and one of the first signs that spring has arrived. You will see her hopping about Mrs. Bumberly's grassy lawn, pulling up worms. Robins build their nests on a low tree branch or in a bush, with the female Robin sitting on the nest of eggs while the male Robin guards the nest from a nearby tree. At night the male robins will all gather together to roost in a tree while the female stays at the nest.

Daffy is the White-breasted Nuthatch who likes to walk upside-down on the large trunk of Mrs. Bumberly's oak tree, with her beak pointing to the ground. A tiny bird, like the finch, nuthatches get their name because of their habit of pushing nuts and acorns with their beak into a tree trunk, storing them for winter. They are very quick little birds. You may not notice them in a tree until they make a quick trip to Mrs. Bumberly's feeder then back up the trunk of the tree again to their hiding place.

LEARN MORE ABOUT BIRDS!

To learn more about birds and to hear recorded sounds of their actual calls and songs, go to: https://allaboutbirds.org and many other sites on the web.

ORDER THIS STORY AS A PHOTO-ILLUSTRATED BOOK!

To order a personalized photo-illustrated book for your child or grandchild, a framed bird photograph, and other bird memorabilia, please contact Linda Conti. And stay tuned for more stories about the adventures of Sweetie Pie and other wonderful birds.

Email: info@abirdslife.org
Website: http://www.abirdslife.org

LUKE PETTIS

Author's Note: This is an excerpt from a novel I am writing that takes inspiration from several post-apocalyptic stories I have read. The most obvious inspiration for my story would have to be Cormac McCarthy's *The Road*. Although, rather than sticking to a more conventional post-apocalyptic setting, I intend to delve into a more niche sub-genre known as fantasy post-apocalyptic. This is more along the lines of works such as Stephen King's *The Dark Tower* series or Jack Vance's *The Dying Earth* series. Admittedly, I also drew inspiration from sources such as anime and video games, as well.

The World After Raxelleon Fell

CHAPTER 1

Year 244: The celestial being simply known as Raxelleon first appears on the northern continent of Planet Georgius.
- Georgius Chronology

Cellus thought, *she's so beautiful, I can't believe I have the important duty of protecting such a lovely girl. It's been years since I've seen any girl, much less a pretty one. I can see how anybody would fall for her, with her long black hair, her shimmering white dress and her green eyes. Not to mention how shapely her body is with her full breasts and thick thighs that I can't help but look at. She's everything a rich human's daughter should look like.*

Cellus was sitting quietly in the stagecoach as it wheeled through a dry, cracked dirt road. He tried to act appropriately while not making the girl in the opposite seat uncomfortable. Cellus was always nervous when talking to girls. It did not help that his father, Maric, was in the driver's seat and could hear everything inside.

He remembered what his father told him before they started this job. *'It doesn't matter if she doesn't appreciate our efforts; what matters is that we deliver her to her home and collect our reward.'*

Cellus did not want to think of her as simply another contract to fulfill. He wanted to make a good impression on her, so she would trust them. However, in the four months he and his father had worked for the girl's family, he had never spoken to her until now. "My name is Cellus. What is your name?"

The girl flinched and looked at him with her eyes wide open. It was the first word spoken since they got into the stagecoach together. "My name is Amelia. I am counting on you to keep me safe throughout this journey." Based on how much Amelia was trembling, Cellus was certain that she was afraid of him more than anything.

"Are you getting hungry by any chance?" He smiled at her hoping she would open up to him.

She stared at him silently.

"Because we could pull over for a quick meal if you want." He tapped on the seat repeatedly.

"I would rather we just keep moving as fast as we can. The sooner I get back to my family's home, the better."

"Is this the first time you have ever left your home?"

"Yes, before now I've never left my family's estate. My father warned me of how dangerous the frontier is."

"Yeah, not too long ago I used to live in my uncle's home and I barely ever got to go outside and talk to anyone either. As I grew up the only person I ever got to play with was my weird cousin Ishtar."

Amelia leaned forward, "What made you leave your home at last?"

"I'm not sure, to be honest. I just remember that one day out of nowhere my dad told me that we had to leave my uncle's home and we were going to work for a human sponsor from then on."

"Did he ever tell you why you had to leave?"

"Not really. Although, I do remember him arguing a lot with my uncle the last few days I lived there." Cellus stared at the wooden frame of the stagecoach.

"Is it okay if I ask you something?" Amelia said.

"Sure, what is it?" *Maybe she trusts me now!*

"Is it true that you are a Shankari?"

Or not. Cellus began to sweat. "What is it you know about the Shankari, precisely?"

Is it so much to ask to meet somebody who sees me for who I am rather than what I am?

"I know that they were once the servants of the black immortal Raxelleon and he created them to be living weapons of war." Amelia shuddered as she mentioned the name of the black immortal.

Cellus had also been stunned when he heard her mention Raxelleon's name. From his people's perspective, Raxelleon had always been a source of reverence, whereas the humans only regarded him with fear. His memory was the only thing the Shankari had to cling to. For after he was defeated, they were left devoid of purpose.

"What else do you know about the Shankari?"

"My parents told me the Shankari deserve to be ostracized by us humans because of the terror they brought to us all those years ago." Her eyes had an accusing look to them.

"Is that what you think of me?" Cellus had his eyes downcast.

"I am a little surprised by how different you are compared to what they told me your kind are supposed to act like." Amelia fidgeted.

"Really? What do you mean by different exactly?" Cellus tried to not get his hopes up.

"I just didn't expect you to be so normal. I mean you don't look scary at all. Not like that other one outside anyway." Amelia indicated Maric.

Cellus sighed, "That's my father you are talking about."

"Oh! I am sorry. I didn't know that." Amelia's face turned red.

The truth was that Cellus did not have much in common with his father Maric. Maric was tall, muscular and had unkempt black hair. Cellus was lean, of average height, and had clean white hair. Their personalities were also different; Maric was strong, intimidating and cynical, whereas Cellus was calm, gentle, and friendly. The only similarity they had was that they both had red eyes, the most distinguishable trait of the warrior caste of the Shankari, the Destroyers.

"Is it okay if I ask you what it's like to be a Destroyer?" Amelia quickly changed the subject.

"I don't really know what to tell you. I mean I'm not really sure there are many differences between us and you humans. I just know that we supposed to be physically stronger than humans. That is, everyone in my clan is very strong, but for some reason I'm not as strong," Cellus explained.

"That's interesting, I suppose."

"But you do understand that my dad and I are different from the perceived image of the Shankari that the Alliance chooses to circulate, right?"

"You mean because the two of you are collaborators?"

Collaborators were Shankari who signed a contract to work for human sponsors.

"No, not just because we are collaborators. I mean that the

Shankari are not all bad. If you just gave us a chance you would see there are good people among us."

"Then why is it that most of your kind chooses not to coexist with humans then?"

"They are just worried they won't receive the same rights as humans do, but that's not true, is it?"

Amelia sat there and stared out the window for more than a minute. After all, this was a subject she had never thought about before.

When Cellus noticed that she was having difficulty answering him, he followed up with, "On second thought, don't worry about it too much. I know it's a very controversial subject right now."

"All right then," Amelia breathed a deep sigh.

"Can you tell me why we are protecting you again? Your father just told us we are supposed to escort you to your family estate, but what are we protecting you from in the first place?" As soon as Cellus asked this, Amelia began to tremble again. "Are people after you because of the spell that is bonded to you?"

This new question caused Amelia to tremble even more. "I don't know what you are talking about." Amelia put her left arm behind her back.

"It's okay, I have a spell of my own right here." Cellus then pulled back his shirt sleeve and revealed the blazing red runic script of an ancient spell bonded to his right arm.

However, this did little to alleviate Amelia's fears: "Why are you showing this to me!?"

"Because I want you to see that you can trust me by showing you my own secret. It would not be fair if I knew your secret and you didn't know mine."

Amelia immediately stopped trembling and her face turned very red. "But you still shouldn't tell somebody you have magic. You know what spellcasters do to obtain more magic, don't you?"

The black immortal and his servants were famous for wielding arcane sorcery in the time of the old Dominion. Ever since his defeat, the secrets of spell-weaving were lost to the sands of time. The only magic that remained in this world came in the form of runic scripts that could be bonded to any person. Due to the diminishing quantity of magic, people everywhere fought over the remaining ancient spells to achieve absolute power.

"Don't worry, as long as we keep each other's spells a secret, there won't be anything we need to worry about," Cellus reassured her.

"I can't promise that I'll keep your spell secret. After all, I didn't ask you to show it to me."

"You don't know anyone who will try to take it from me, do you?"

Amelia did not answer the question.

"Am I that foolish for hoping we could be friends because we share a secret?"

"I-I didn't say that you are foolish, I-I just wasn't certain of your intentions, that's all." Amelia's face turned red again as she said this.

"You don't really think I am going to try to take your magic away, do you?"

"That's what all other spellcasters out there are doing to each other."

"Well I'm going to be the one who will keep you safe from all the others. Don't you doubt it for a second!"

"Are you that experienced of a fighter?" Amelia was both charmed and hopeful.

"My dad has trained me the best he could since I was six years old, plus I have this spell that can shoot fireballs at will. What about you? What can your spell do?"

"I have telescopic vision which lets me see through walls up to fifty meters."

"That's...What does that mean?" Cellus asked.

She paused for a moment and said, "Well, I can see far away objects as if they're right in front of me..." Amelia looked out the stagecoach's right window, then her face tightened...

"They're here. *They're after me!*"
CHAPTER 2

Year 342: The Great Purge: over 5,000,000 people have fallen at the hands of Raxelleon's Destroyers.
- Georgius Chronology

Maric sat in the stagecoach's driving seat. Behind him, his son Cellus was inside keeping watch over their employer's daughter. Riding to his left was Adrian the guard captain of their escort. Like the rest of the Freege family guardsmen, he was wearing a beige trench coat and carrying a double-barreled rifle.

Adrian spoke up, "You better know what you are doing, Destroyer. It wasn't easy to convince the master to not only allow you to drive the stagecoach, but to also let your son accompany his daughter, Lady Amelia, inside."

Maric was quick to retort, "Well, who else is capable of fending off danger like I can? Besides, it's not as if the girl ever gets to talk to anyone close to her age anyway."

"Be that as it may, I don't need to remind you that our master has not been very satisfied with your recent performance. You may have no trouble with defeating our enemies, but your constant disregard of orders has repeatedly jeopardized every operation you have participated in. Suffice to say, this will be your last chance to serve our master in a proper manner. Otherwise, both you and your son will be sent back to the camps where we first found you."

Maric shuddered after Adrian finished. He tried to get his mind off his current predicament when he noticed that one of the guards riding in the front of the stagecoach was spying on them. When the guard realized that Maric was onto him, he quickly turned away and galloped ahead.

Heh. Of course, they're intimidated by me, I bet that deep down these smalltime household guards know that they will quickly become obsolete now that their rich human masters are starting to hire Shankari Destroyers as mercenaries. They know they can't compete with our fighting style or our naturally sturdier bodies. Why else would they be giving me all this shit? Maric thought to himself.

Maric turned back to Adrian, "It seems as though you are the only one here who can look me in the eye."

"There are few out here who haven't heard of the atrocities your people committed back in the days of the old Dominion. However, I know that you, like us, are a fallible mortal being. But, that doesn't change the fact that my master still thinks of you as a large investment that he has yet to see as profitable." Adrian eyed Maric intently.

"I spent the last twenty years of my life studying the ancient art of combat that my clan's elders have preserved for centuries. This was the only way I could impress a human client into allowing me to enter his service."

"Ensuring your own freedom was one thing, but I am impressed that you were able to convince my master to take in your son as well."

"It was too dangerous for Cellus to be in the camps anymore, besides as long as I can persuade the Freeges that my son is serving as my apprentice, they will learn the benefit of having two Destroyers in their service."

"You say that, but I'm not convinced that your son has the makings of a warrior at all. I have served with many soldiers with traits such as aggression, pride and valor, but I do not see these in your son."

"He will learn these qualities in due time, He'll soon find that he must understand how to fight if he wants to survive in this world we live in."

"It takes more than understanding through necessity for one to become a warrior."

"This is a matter for me work on, not for you," Maric snapped at him.

"Regardless, are you certain you are fine with becoming a collaborator? They say that most Shankari not only refuse to work alongside humans in any way, but they are antagonistic towards those who do agree to work for us."

"I'm doing this for the good of my child. Nobody could possibly fault me for that."

"Well, if you both can keep the master's daughter safe, I don't think either of you will have anything to worry about there."

"That's another thing, what are the Freeges thinking, sending their only daughter out to the Disputed lands like this? We were lucky we didn't have any trouble while we brought her to that excavation site, but there's no telling what could happen before we return to the estate."

"It's not for us to question our master's will, we simply need to see it carried out. As long as I am here guiding you there is no need for concern for our journey," Adrian reassured.

Maric continued to brood over their situation until he remembered to assess his surroundings. He checked his own attire which was made up of a long black coat which covered his scimitar as well as the four spells he had bonded to himself.

Then he gazed around at the four other guardsmen who worked for the Freege family. Each of them was riding mutated oxen that were the same as the ones pulling the stagecoach. Then he heard two of the guards talking to each other from their position behind the stagecoach.

"Are you sure it's a good idea that we leave that young Destroyer alone with the master's daughter? If you ask me, it's only a matter of time until he forces himself on that girl."

"I say we take both out regardless. That way we'll have a bigger slice of the reward once we bring the girl back to the Freege Estate."

Maric was certain that they knew he could hear them and they did not care that he could.

Who do these human bastards think they are anyway? First, they managed to defeat our master Raxelleon, and usurped our position as controllers of this world. Then they branded us monsters and sent us to those concentration camps. Now they must doubt us at every turn as if we are the ones responsible for the current state the world is in.

"Hey, knock it off both of you! You won't receive any salary if you don't stop mouthing off and start to focus on doing your duty!" Adrian yelled at the two rear guards before Maric could say anything to them.

After Adrian was through shouting, Maric gazed off into the distance and observed the land in every direction. He saw a barren wasteland with all trace of vegetation obliterated ages ago. Their whole journey took them countless miles across endless stretches of rock, sand and ash-riddled dirt unfit for habitation.

"Can I ask you something else?" Maric continued conversing with Adrian.

"What is it?"

"How often do you come across plants in human cities?"

"Not very often. All forms of greenery are more precious than magic or any other artifact left over from the old Dominion. I have only seen a few plants back at the master's estate. Only rich families like the Freeges can afford plants for a personal garden. But practically all crop farming is being monopolized by the governing body in each territory. All the remaining human countries are in constant conflict with each other over the remaining resources left in our world."

"I thought as much," Maric responded somberly.

"Are the Shankari not allowed to grow plants of their own?"

"I can remember the stories our elders told us about when the world used to be full of green things such as trees, bushes and other plants that grew many things to eat. They told us of endless fields of grass that made the ground soft and moist instead of always hard and dry everywhere. However, back in the camps there is hardly enough fertile soil back for us to grow anything. Barely any of us Destroyers knew much about farming in the first place. That was always something the Preservers handled for us. As a result, there was hardly enough food for everyone in the camps. Many of us formed gangs who constantly fought each other over who would get the food. If my older brother had not been the leader of the biggest gang, I probably would not have been able to acquire enough food for both me and Cellus."

Then Maric and the rest heard a scream from the inside of the stagecoach. He opened the stagecoach window behind him and asked, "What's going on in there?"

"I don't know! She just started screaming all of a sud-"

"You see! I told you he was going to touch her!" One of the guards had cut Cellus off.

"Would you shut the hell up?!" Maric snapped at him.

"My Lady, what is the matter?" Adrian asked while ignoring everybody else.

"We need to move faster! They're going to be here in just another minute!" Amelia yelled.

"I knew this would happen! That boy of yours couldn't possibly be in there that long without trying something with her!" Another guard yelled while brandishing his gun and pointing it at Maric.

"Stand down, all of you!" Adrian was doing his best to stay in control of the situation.

This whole journey was going just fine until something like this happened... Who am I kidding? This was going to happen no matter what.

Maric was reaching for his sword until he noticed something to the right of the stagecoach flash in the distance. An ethereal missile hurtled towards their position.

"They're here!!" Amelia was screaming at the top of her lungs.

Maric pulled hard on the reins to bring the stagecoach to a halt. The missile blasted away the two front guards on impact.

"Dad! What are you doing?!" Cellus was surprised by the sudden lurch from both the explosion and the stagecoach slowing down.

"What the hell did you do to Clark and Anthony!?" One of the guards from the rear shouted as he galloped closer to the stagecoach.

"By the power of the black immortal we shall claim what is rightfully ours!" Three men appeared from the left of the stagecoach and quickly cut down the two rear guards.

These men were wild looking, wielding sabers and half

dressed in broiled leather outfits with messy hair and covered in tattoos from head to toe. They were all riding mutated hyenas that were closing in on the stagecoach.

Maric unsheathed his scimitar and parried a blow from a marauder who had reached him first. They traded blow after blow until Maric slashed the raider across his chest and he fell off his mount.

"Take this!" Adrian fired his rifle at the second marauder who approached them. The marauder was hit in the head and fell off his mount.

"Why don't you try to stop me now!" The third marauder had climbed to the top of the stagecoach and had raised his saber above his head intending to stab through the roof.

"*Gatij!*"

Maric responded by throwing his sword. He used a spell to guide his blade's trajectory, and it hurled towards the man and sliced through his neck before it returned to Maric like a boomerang. Afterwards, the raider fell off the stagecoach and the hyenas scattered as a result.

"Listen to me, Cellus! I need you to come up here and take the reins while I chase down the rest of them. I have no doubt they are from the Orgal Clan." Maric yelled into the stagecoach.

Cellus climbed through the stagecoach window and took the reins from Maric. "Are you going to go after them now, Dad?"

"That is correct. Just make sure to cover me. But be careful of how you aim."

"Wait, are you seriously going to go after them all by yourself?" Adrian was still responding to everything happening so far.

"Just stay with the stagecoach until I have this taken care of."

Maric jumped off the stagecoach and started to run to intercept the main body of the clan marauders who were coming.

"*Mabail!*"

He then utilized one of his other spells to increase his speed to a degree faster than the inbound hyena riders were moving. He dashed towards the raiders in blinding speed, jumped, decapitated one of them, and landed on the ground in one flowing motion.

Another raider charged towards Maric, but he was ready for him.

"*Gatij!*"

Maric tossed his sword at this marauder as well. It pierced through the raider like an arrow, then it sprung from his chest and returned to Maric's hand.

The rest of the marauders were awestruck by the strike Maric delivered to their companion. Their leader spoke up, "After him! He's wielding Magic! We shall punish one of his fallen servants, take his power, and demonstrate that we are more deserving of it!"

That figures. The only reason the Freege family allowed Cellus and I to have magic in the first place is because they knew it would make the raiders to go after us first. Not that it did their household guards any good, that is. At least I can use this to draw their attention away from the stagecoach.

Maric kept his focus on the rest of the riders and was relieved when he saw that all fifteen of them were wielding sabers instead of any projectile weapons. Then he noticed that the leader had started to chant his own spell. Then he remembered the long-range magic from before that he narrowly avoided.

"*Faayar!!*"

A flash came from behind Maric, then a large fireball blazed across his left flank and exploded just in front of the riders.

That was close, but at least Cellus knows how to give proper cover fire. He didn't get the leader. I'll have to take care of him next before he is able to finish chanting his spell.

"I'll back you up as well, comrade!" Adrian galloped towards Maric while firing his rifle.

"I thought I told you to stay with the stagecoach!" Maric yelled behind him.

"It's fine. After all, we've nearly got them," Adrian halted his steed fifty yards behind Maric.

"*Shikhandi!*"

Before either of them were ready, the leader of the marauders had finished casting another ethereal missile.

"Take evasive action!" Maric shouted. As he was about to leap out of the way, he noticed that the slow-moving comet-like missile was not heading in either of their directions. He followed its trajectory and saw where it was going.

"*Oh shit! It's heading straight for the stagecoach!*" Maric had never screamed this loud before in his life.

I can't believe it! I worked so hard to try and care for Cellus his whole life, but now I'm about to lose him right before my eyes and I can't stop it! I should have never left him alone back there! How will I ever be able to face Sigrun now?!

The gravity of the situation had Maric paralyzed with terror.

"Fear not, my friend! For the glory of the Freege family I will fulfill my duty as their loyal servant!" Adrian galloped towards the impending projectile.

"What can you possibly do to stop it?!"

"The only thing I can!" Adrian collided with the missile.

Maric just stood there stunned as he watched the explosion engulf the only honorable human he had ever known. He turned around and glared at the remaining five marauders. As they gazed at the fury that was evident in his red eyes, they knew they did not stand a chance against him now that they used the rest of their magic. As a result, all five of them turned and started to make their retreat.

Maric gave chase to the Marauders. "*Get back here, damn it! I swear I won't rest until I gut every one of you!*"

R. DAVID DRUCKER

Author's Note: The five poems I offer you are based on my struggle to understand the loss of most of the women who have been most intimately involved in my life, one on the operating table, one by suicide, and the rest of natural causes. Some of my work of the past three years has been so raw, I have hesitated to expose them to anyone but the few faithful readers to whom I have sent everything I've written in the past three years. Nor have I pulled back the curtain on other obsessions of mine—the sea and sailing, pre-Conquest Mexico and Central America, Buddhist and Sufi approaches to the meaning of life. They have generated their own poems which are not represented here. This is not the place for them, although I couldn't resist including two poems with the sea as the source of metaphors for love and attachment.

You should be warned that my "voice" in these poems is often addressed to those lovers I have lost. Sometimes I see one or two or even three of them out of the corner of my eye on a back porch moonlit night, popping out of doorways, or simply lounging in a chair I'm just about to sit in. Suicide and how it may be prevented is often on my mind. My loss has made me sensitive to the loss other survivors have suffered. This forms the core of my elegy to "Scared Rabbit."

My losses have caused me to become more self-reflective, although I am constantly reminded by myself and others not nearly enough. "Even Mean Boys . . ." as its last couplet implies, is more than a tad autobiographical.

Finally, despite enduring a heavy dose of grief and loss these past three years, I like to think I've still retained a sense of humor. Thus, "Who Am I About To Turn Into Next" is pure fantasy, but based on the salmon [and wine!] obsession of a new friend who thoroughly approves of the poem. The octopus poem grew out of my fascination with Sy Montgomery's work observing them at the New England Aquarium in preparation for writing her recent book. The fact that I have lost three intimately close loves in three years and that the octopus has three hearts and only lives for three years bonds me to them as a metaphor for my journey of loss.

But, fear not, dear reader. These are playful poems as well as sad. Don't be afraid to enjoy them!

Five Poems

Even Mean Boys Can Learn To Love Themselves
And, When They Do, There's Love In Them For You

Mean boys don't believe you can break their hearts.
They've broken them so long ago themselves,
they can't remember when they went so mean.

All mean boys have forgotten they have hearts,
so suffer just as much as their victims,
but have a funny way to express it –
funny peculiar, not funny ha ha.

All mean boys aren't heartless all the time.

Sometimes on a cold morning in their souls,
mean boys cry tears for those they have betrayed.
They wake up from their dreams, breaking a sweat,
but check their swing when they're not ready yet
to let themselves remember why they fight,
resist the urge to open their closed hearts,
stare themselves down in a broken mirror
not seeing the fugitive there is them.

Mean boys would rather stage a scene than stay
calm, cool, and collected enough to play
fair with themselves to show themselves they dare
to care for themselves if no one's looking.

When some mean boys go to bed every night,
they tuck in early, to avoid the fright
they might feel if they looked inside themselves
instead of bullying everyone else.

Mean boys sometimes don't mean to be that way,
but may take years to liberate themselves.

Truth to tell, they're like all first time lovers –
don't recognize themselves until they learn
how hard it is to come to love yourself
when you've been a mean boy most of your life.

Take this recovered mean boy's word for it –
it can be done if you live long enough.

Who Am I About To Turn Into Now?

" . . . be careful, or you'll become what you eat."
For Laurie-Beth Robbins

Recently, I've discovered a new shore
pregnant with the promise of fresh salmon.

Eating berries turned me into a bear
without having to be a cannibal,
yet, I'm feeling an old habit return,
though eating those I crave will transform me
in basic ways I can anticipate.

I was born Bear, to Bear I have returned.

But, in adolescence, I thought cow thoughts,
transfigured by hamburgers, liver, steak,
succulent beef stew, and – as a treat – tongue.
Milkshakes rounded out my cow repertoire
and, in summer, endless scoops of ice cream.
I felt I was indistinguishable
from your average, cow fed, neighborhood Bear
occasionally letting methane gas
confirm to me I was part of the herd.

I escaped a cow fate more artlessly
than by any attention to detail.
Sure, I'd still eat ice cream every summer,
a burger and fries every now and then,
but no longer enough to be cow-like
because in my twenties pig meat was king.

Pig fed my slovenly eating habits –
bacon and eggs morning, noon, and weekends,

whole pig roasted in an open fire pit,
sausages, scrapple, and baby back ribs,
lard fried pizzas. All around my kitchen
plastic, metal, and wood piglets gathered
squeallesly proclaiming me a sinner
to any visitor who chose to see –
brought me close to turning into a pig.

That close call remade me an omnivore.
Once more I grew to like vegetables, nuts,
various kinds of herbs and spices, rice,
and I did develop a fruit passion.
I returned to my primitive food roots,
living more and more each day like a Bear
willing to let the cow/pig in me die.

I lived this way for many years in caves,
contented, for the most part, with berries,
honey, or succulent bugs I scavenged
throughout my comforting forest home base.

I hardly ever fished the well-stocked streams
except in the fall when the salmon spawned.

Each lonely day went by like the others,
reinforcing my bear-like character.

If I'd been hibernating as I should,
I would never have awakened to good,
fierce carnivore reactions once again.

Emerging from the early morning mist,
barely discernable from my cave's mouth,
a fierce warrior salmon princess dares

me to care about her strange entourage,
her magnificent boat, and eight willing
salmon as feisty as the princess herself.

"Take. Eat. For these are the fish I have brought
for you and for many to bring you health."

Every fiber in me hears her calling
to eat salmon freely or die trying.

It's been less than a week, yet I worry
I will be transformed right here on this shore,
might be swept off my feet by her fierce lure
she casts with wild abandon at my feet.

"Hey! Come on in Bear, the water is fine . . .
just right for salmon and a glass of wine
by the fireplace. Want to go fishing?"

What If The Four Of Us Lived In The Sea Entwined In A Mutual Fantasy?

For my three loves, Mary, Lori, and Suz,
with a joyful squeeze for Sy Montgomery.

If I had the soul of an octopus,
I'd always choose which tentacle to use
based on its characteristics . . . shy ones
for opening up shrinking violets . . .
powerful ones for me to match my grip
with an attractive octopus cougar . . .
and a compassionate one, or sad one,
to communicate with chemical tact
that would not turn me red when excited.

I'd tender one of them to one of you,
never interfering with the others' needs.

My three hearts would let me get up to speed
more responsively than you'd imagine,
if you desired it, while I'd sip tea
with our other two chatty companions.

My quivering suckers would savor you
while the others fed fish to my armpit
for the shear thrill of seeing me engaged
in something besides receptivity
to others needs all day long and all night.

My new fluidity might give a fright
to kids and small dogs before they knew me,
but they'd soon get over it, let me love
them if they'd been good little girls and boys –
or small dogs for that matter.

                    I'd splash them
just for the fun of it and, I would hope,
they would take to me as I took to them
so I could live out my three year life span
with equanimity and unafraid.

The Scared Rabbit, Scott Hutchinson, Has Died
On Wednesday Of This Week Of Suicide

"Let him not have written his songs in vain"
with thanks to CBC's As It Happens

Silently, lads search the hills. All Scotland
waits with baited breath his reappearance.
Even the cynical give it a rest
thinking of what worried neighbors might say.

But for his lyrics, he'd appeared o.k.:
"How are you doing today?

                                    "Pretty good.
Six out of a possible ten, I'd say,"
his reply to a reporter's question.

The usual gloom of the windswept moors
seemed uncharacteristically restrained.
Sun tried to hide, embarrassed to be seen,
but was observed. Larks at the break of day
remained silent. They had nothing to say
to alleviate the hurt of heartbreak.

This had to be endured for three whole days
until, unressurected, Scared Rabbit
was discovered sleeping on a hillside
bedecked by every wild flower that grows,
his body unattended, deathly still,
sleeping that sleep that never awakens
the dreamer when he has finished dreaming
and takes a permanent turn for the worse.

Only three days ago he had been asked,

"How are you feeling today?"

                                          "Pretty good!
Six out of a possible ten, I'd say,"
he'd replied with his usual humor
masking his joy-killer, depression, well.

Reader, I write this Pedestrian Verse
not to show off my skill in a perverse
attempt to cut short another poet
who has just managed to do that himself.

Anyone with half a head should have thought
something was up when Rabbit disappeared,
gone with not so much as a by your leave.

But no one noticed birds began to grieve,
leaving off their cheery migratory
patterns of avian conversation,
to intone wordless first hints of a dirge
before the awful truth was uncovered
when Scared Rabbit's body was discovered.

Friday's The Loneliest Night Of The Week

Written alongside the love nest we shared, dear Lori.
May you have forgiven me.

My Darling, hold my hand and come inside.
Let us pretend we have nothing to hide
this joy filled night . . . no thoughts of suicide.

I, your sommelier, will be by your side
into the wee hours of the morning
should you wish to imbibe.

      You have been warned.
I am your shadow. I will not be denied
this remarriage, knowing my foolish pride
won't drive a stake in the heart of our love.

There's so much more I have to tell you, Love,
what I'll do to protect you. I will shore
you up when I feel you falling, restore
the laughter that attracted me to you,
Gorgeous Girl.

    It's useless to implore
you to come inside . . . too many Fridays
have come and gone with neither of us home.

Our happy Fridays are now forgotten
by this brick and mortar that held our love
safe from a cruel, uncomprehending world
'til the Friday on which you felt betrayed
by your lover who didn't seem to care
whether you lived or died more than you did.

195 of the Denim Poets Society

This Friday, I wish that I would have stayed
here instead of playing the part I played.

CLETUS CAPITANO

Author's Note: Digging into my old kit bag, I pull out a short story, a poem, a piece of flash fiction, and a comic sketch. It's my day job, such as it is.

Encounter on Highway 49

"Don't come back now, ya hear?" said the sheriff, his chaw-filled cheek bulbed up like a puffer fish. My bus was just coming round the corner.

I was an acquisition agent for the Smithsonian. I'd been forty days in the delta, scouring the land for vintage crop-dusters, hammer mills, cultivators, planters, plows. I was in Clarksdale to wrestle the last known H-10H, a mechanized cotton picker, from hard-selling Willie Hopkins.

"You federal men," said a deputy, swiveling his dubious

head to project a squirt of tobacco juice, "you ain't never gonna convince old Hopkins to give up that damn relic. He don't even care that everybody's got six-row pickers now that'll gobble up a hundred acres a day. Hush, you're dreaming, boy."

"No, deputy," I said, tipping my hat to the sheriff, "I *will* swing back: I believe to my soul Willie's judging to write the ole Smith into his will."

"Hell, that man'll never die," said the sheriff. "He's old as the earth, 'bout five thousand years. Ain't but one thing older than that gray Negro."

"What's that?"

"His pappy!"

The bus pulled in with a kick of dust that billowed down the tired, sun-settled street. It sat there calmly idling: white roof, yellow skirt, and bands of green framing the headstrong windows. As the accordion doors squeaked open I was clinched by a man, skinny as a celery stick. "*Gooch!*" I squawked. Our embrace lingered.

Gooch slapped me on the back. "Yer coming back this weekend t'barrelhouse, eh, brother?"

I'd been sitting in with a local band, blowing blues harp. I guess they kinda liked me.

The driver, scratchy and road-worn, mauled the gearshift, saying, "Doncha worry, Gooch. He'll be back. Why d'ya think ole Willie's holdin' out?"

I winked at the driver, noting his new cap and, for some reason, his badge number: 2857. The first four rows were filled with fifty-pound sacks of High Grade Diatomaceous Earth. I passed them and took a seat next to an old mossback in a ginger suit which must have once been presentable. He wore a silver beard, ancient and wispy. His hands trembled slightly while he slept, as if active in their own dreams.

Just outside of Whitehead he woke.

"Ever had such a mighty fine sleep?" he asked, as if I'd been privy to his slumber.

"Yes," I said, reflexively, "once...along the river."

He nodded as if it were his memory, too. I don't know why, but I gripped his hand, maybe for pity, maybe for strength.

"Know any good traveling games?" he said.

"Uh. Yes. Firsts and lasts is a good one."

"How's that?"

"Name the first or last of something: like the last day of your first job."

"My first job lasted seven days whole, and I only worked but six of'm."

"Crafty!"

"Spent the whole day stringing lights. Lamps of every which way. Next day built up a mess of levees. You know, to divide the waters."

I gestured as if the game were better played at a different hour. I tried to look preoccupied.

The bus thumped and juddered along. I turned quickly to the pages of a curled magazine left behind. Poems, puzzles, lore. Sometime later I snorted, "Aw, Jupiter!"

"Some bothering words there?" said the old man.

"Somebody musta really liked Robert Frost." I raised the magazine. "*Fire & Ice* was supposed to be right there." And I slapped the leaf. Someone had torn out half a page where the verse had been.

"Let's have a see." He took the magazine, wet two fingers, closed the covers and handed it back with a look of nostalgia. I ran my finger down the page, perfectly restored.

Somewhat unplucked, I asked, "Whudja do the rest of the week?"

"Oh, seeded some grass, planted some trees. Stocked a few ponds, did a little husbandry. Printed up a calendar." Then he added, shyly, "did a little matchmakin', too. It was all good."

"And on the last day?"

"Tilted back in a hammock!"

About ten miles from Yazoo City there came a mighty *thump* and the bus fishtailed onto the shoulder. The driver stopped and circled the bus, swearing up holy creation when he saw the blown tire. Passengers emptied out into the foxtail grass. I sat on a honeysuckle fence. When no one was looking, the old man moved to the shredded tire.

He wet two fingers and lay hands on the face of rubber. Then he joined me; my mouth was dry, and all I could do was watch the driver scratch himself silly. Three minutes later, back on the road, the old mossback whispered, "I got a chile back in Clarksdale. I look in on'm from time to time."

"Just one?"

He looked out over the dry brown land, his face an array of longing and dashed-down hope.

"No, I got others. All along this route."

"You must ride often."

"I hardly ever step off this oil-burner."

I looked up at the sky, blue as a cold-fevered sapphire. Not one cloud.

"These farmers need rain, bad," I said.

"True."

He wet two fingers, like a grizzled pitcher on a raised diamond.

Off to the west, a child's kite fluttered high in the firmament. And from it grew a continent-sized thunderhead. It rose and flowered.

"Sometimes," he said wistfully, "I think about startin' all over."

He gripped my hand for a moment, maybe for strength, maybe for pity.

I slid open the ornery window and felt the rain upon my face. And mindlessly repeated what I hadn't heard, "Yeah, *sometimes.*"

He let out a heartsick breath and turned to look through the sheets of rain far out into the sweep of that territory; after taking again my hand into his, he sighed, saying, "Nay...often."

STRING THEORY

She's out walking in space,
her thoughts send her Alcatraz way,
but all she wants to feel
is the pulse beneath her feet
            twenty Hertz through-the-earth

She keeps her ear to the ground,
the growl and the grumble and the grace
notes of sandbags and mud flats,
            Blue globe, nickel core
she paces the power lines that sag overhead,
she's got a feeling for strings
            round wound, long scale

Elephants in the lowlands,
whales at the bottom of the sea,
Mingus, Carol Kaye & the bowman,
we all dig the deep frequencies

She connects with tom-tom and friends,
venturing, centurying extended december jams,
            swing low, swing deep
she's got a theory 'bout strings

She's found her way, walking in place
letting the earth pulse beneath
            Blue globe, nickel core
she rides ancient wavelengths,

rumbling down subsonic alleys,
            round wound, long scale
string theory is what brings us together
            twenty Hertz through-the-earth

Elephants in the lowlands,
whales at the bottom of the sea,
Mingus, Carol Kaye & the bowman,
we all dig the deep frequencies

Swing low
Blue globe
nickel core
round wound
long scale
twenty Hertz through-the-earth
string theory is what holds us together

The Emissary of East Greenwich

In my study I have before me a roulette wheel, an almanac of place names, an unabridged dictionary, my typewriter of course, a contraption that tells me the temperature of any city in the world, and the current metropolitan telephone book, fat as a lamb.

I've covered the numbers of the roulette wheel with letters, doubling up on the eleven most common: *e-t-a-o-i-n-s-h-r-d-l*. A sequence, by the way, which produces some delightful anagrams: *thin ordeals, ideal thorns, nailed short.*

I like to begin my routine immediately after breakfast, when the day is fresh. But, for diversity's sake, I'll work any hour. Day or night, as long as my subjects are home and, most importantly, unsuspecting.

Perhaps you're not familiar: let me explain. One spin of the wheel, the ball drops, I have a letter. I go then to that letter's head in my almanac and choose, more or less at random, the name of a town or city. Once chosen, I obtain the current temperature of that place. In the dictionary I locate the page corresponding to the temperature and run my finger down the leaf until the moment my second breath begins and there arrive at my word.

I compose a brief passage in my register using that word, for this is a venerable task that demands an account.

Now, with the same number, I consult the telephone directory, and—using the following calculus—I arrive at a name. Watch.

Here, come with me, I'll show you.

We knock at the door of—today, remember, it is Mr. Arthur Kinard, seller of stainless steel kitchenware and upright vacuums.

Mr. Kinard answers and I raise my .38 Special and pull the trigger.

The man stands wide-eyed and unsteady. He swallows. Then again.

I smile and spin the cylinder of the pistol so that he can see that five of the six chambers are empty.

And I say, "Be glad. The Lord has spared you today."

Now we return to the study.

Holden Caulfield Prepares Benedictory Remarks for the 2017 Inauguration

On the 42nd floor of the Pencey Point Center for Assisted Living, the quintessential figure of adolescent angst, Mr. H. M. Caulfield, now 83 years old, sits on the edge of a plastic leather armchair, looking fretfully out into the free-thinking canyons of mid-town Manhattan. His reverie is on the 60-foot waterfall at Trump Tower; he lingers, musing on its soothing, almost sanctified opulence, then turns to his roommate.

"For chrissakes, Stradlater, pay attention will you. I've got to finish this speech."

"Never thought I'd see you banging out copy on an iPad."

"Not an iPad; it's a Surface Pro. Microsoft. Gotta change with the times, old sport."

"*Change* is right—and you're the living triumph. I still can't believe you're supporting that lousy bastard... Some swing."

"You never heard of the Apostle Paul? Murdering Christians left and right. Then, poof! Now, *there's* a conversion."

"Yeah, *but he went the other way*. You on the other hand...."

"How 'bout Anne Rice, then: blood-sucking atheist to pious fundamentalist."

"We're talking politics here, Holden."

"OK... Well, Adam Sandler did in fact back Rudy Giuliani."

"I thought the disciples annoyed the hell out of you, anyway?"

"Well, if you want to know the truth. I grew up."

The nimble but ripened Caulfield frantically rummages through a case of DVDs, bringing out copies of "Rebel Without a Cause" and "Easy Rider," thrusting them close to the face of his roommate, squealing: "Who was more counterculture than Dennis Hopper, eh? Conservatives hated that libtard with a passion. Am I wrong? Yet..."

"I know, I know. Reagan turned him batshit Republican."

"Right! And he voted for *both* Bushes. Became a real defender of the faith. So you've got to respect...."

"...fanatics?"

"He saw the light. Just as I..."

"I think that light came from the magic mushrooms you dropped with Hopper and Nicholson at, where was it....?"

"Psilocybin...at D.H. Lawrence's grave. I recanted all that pap. I was young."

"Why you doing this, Holden?"

"Because for seventy years I've been waiting for an emancipator, the one true savior, a fearless hero who *tells it like it is*. You take the goddam phoniest bastard that ever lived and Trump: well, he's the exact unmitigated opposite. The paragon of authenticity. The nonesuch of probity. He's pure dope."

"No debate there."

"Stradlater, the man's bigger than Gatsby. So, so, so....*grand*."

"Grand! You used to puke whenever anybody spoke that word."

"Progress, Strad. All a flowering. You ought to read a little Tony Robbins."

"Mr. Antolini would have a hemorrhage if he ever heard..."

"What I need to do *now* is focus on this speech. I don't want the crowd to be yelling '*Digression!*' every lousy five seconds."

"You used to hate it when people stuck to the point all the time."

"One of the reasons I love Trump. He *never* sticks to the point."

"Never *makes* a point."

"Recall I flunked Oral Expression; well, this one I wanna ace."

"You're still miffed at what Mailer said about you. You just want a platform to..."

"That '*greatest mind ever to stay in prep school*' crap? Mailer's a loser. Third-string flop."

"Faulkner stung you, too. What he said about buzzing inside

the glass wall of your own tumbler. That hurt..."

"Crap it did! The *"Art of the Deal"* outsold anything Mr. Yoknapatawpha ever scribbled. Bare-footed socialist hayseed!"

"Where's all the hostility coming from, Holden? How'd you ever get zipped up with this guy anyway?"

"I love golf. You *know* I've been golfing since I was ten. I'm out at a club in Palm Beach, teeing off. Then out of the corner of my eye I see this guy sitting on a cart about a hundred and fifty yards away—his hair was so red. For some reason I started thinking about my favorite book, 'Return of the Native.' The only book that ever knocked me out more was 'The Art of the Comeback.'"

"I thought you loved Ring Lardner best?"

"It's a new world, Strad."

"Huh?"

"So I see that this guy sitting on the cart, all decked out, is Trump himself. I always thought about how when you're done reading a sumptuously clinquant book, you wish the author was a stupendous friend of yours and you could just phone him up whenever you felt like it. Well, there he was! The author of 'Think Big and Kick Ass.' I dropped my clubs and just walked right up to him, all Nick Carraway like."

"His hair's not actually red....tends more toward orangutan."

"We just clicked. Talked a blue streak about everything he ever put his hand to. He invited me to the clubhouse. Had some drinks. Then ended up back in his residence, playing Daifugo and talking 'bout how America was going down the goddam toilet. You wouldn't believe who else was there. Roger Clemens, Mel Gibson, Paul McCartney and all these Marie Antoinette-types just floating everywhere, serving lobster frittatas and foie gras. I'm not saying there wasn't affluence or privilege or ego. Why pretend? For chrissakes they had a special set of teak cubicles just for stowing everyone's driving gloves. Once you got to *know* these people, though, they were the most goddam genuine customers you ever met. They were *real*. You never saw McCartney wear a monocle, have you....but at Trump's he could.

Because he was free to be his *authentic self.* And Clemens could open up real vulnerable. Like a tale he told about this female reporter stumbling into the locker-room and catching him *au naturel.* She shrieked, "Oh, God!" And good old Clemens calmed her right down, saying: "Just call me Roger, honey!" It was *sooo* original! Now, there's nothing *intrinsically* wrong with narcissists. As long as they're true to themselves, that's what I learned that night. Except for Dennis Miller. Asshole from beginning to end."

"We have a point of agreement."

"Everyone went to bed and Donald and I stayed up, like camp buddies, shooting the shit all night long. We both positively adored William F. Buckley. Just before we hit the sack he drew me close and whispered all maharishi-like: '*All you have to do is say something nobody understands and they'll do practically anything you want'm to.*' That sonofabitch—haven't I always had the *very same idea!*"

"So that was rapture enough to go to the devil?"

"No. It wasn't till the next day when I got a good look at Trump's luggage. *That* was the corker. The man has the peachiest suitcases in the goddam solar system. Satchels, steamers, totes, trunks, trolleys... Made Louis Vuitton's bags look like Dollar Store close-outs. I swooned. They had to bring out the smelling salts."

"And for his suitcases you're writing the benediction for his Inaugural?"

"Doncha *get it?* For chrissakes his kits were covered in pony skin, porosus crocodile, pearled rayfish, you name it...."

"Let me hear the opening."

"Haven't gotten that far yet. I got snippets. I'm working with *images.*"

"The ceremony's *tomorrow!*"

"I figure this, Roomie: everyone still knows me as the most terrific liar they ever saw. It's appalling. If I'm on my way to buy a newspaper and some bonehead asks where I'm going, I'm liable to say I'm headin' to the hippodrome."

"Jesus, Antolini'd be spinning in his grave."

"Follow me. I kinda start out roasting Trump, but like I was serious. Saying some kooky stuff. Remember the Seinfeld episode 'The Opposite?' Knowing me, everybody will take my *reverse* meaning."

"Knowing you?"

"Well, old chap, I *am* the headliner of a book that's sold 65 million copies."

"True."

"So, I open with this bit about how even on the highest throne in the world we still only sit on our own bottom. With one exception.... Then I get the crowd to go raving mad yelling, *'TRUMP! TRUMP!'*"

"You're 83 years old, Holden..."

"So I go to a crack about him leading a life so not to be embarrassed to sell the family parrot to the town gossip. But, see, *that's his virtue.* All of his kinks and defects are *already* out there. And nobody gives a damn. Except his impotence; he confided to me—don't say a word."

"You're gonna do a stand-up routine for the Inauguration?"

"It's theology, Strad. I thought I'd even insult the audience a bit... Using Churchill's line, ya know, about the greatest lesson in life is to know that even fools sometimes get it right.... Voters."

"Not so dignified, Holden."

"*Dignity?* Hell, no...! That's the whole point! Dignity is the opposite of everything Trump stands for! It's a new era, and the new virtue is being the most execrable savage scurvy *truth*-teller alive."

"Lord..."

"Finally, the last line: I introduce him as the cock who thinks the sun rises just to hear him crow. Then he comes to the podium, still aquiver with my remarks, his ruby locks all standing on end."

"So you're not going to praise Caesar?"

"Strad, I'm crazy. I swear to God I am."

Functus Officio

CONTRIBUTORS:

Gillian Mary Crawford Aguilar was born in Pinner, Middlesex, a suburb of London, England. She lived there into her early twenties until she came to the United States in 1963 and later became an American citizen. She received her MAT from Tufts University in Medford, Massachusetts, and taught German and French for ten years at Belmont High School in Massachusetts, as well as at her home. She has four children and seven grandchildren, all of whom play a very important role in her life. She wanted to share her life with them and some special friends now that she has reached her eighties. She enjoyed very much looking back and remembering so many incidents and special occasions in a rich and varied life. She lives in the lovely little seacoast city of Portsmouth, New Hampshire, where she is very active meeting with friends, watercolor painting, walking and exercising, acting in a senior theatre group, playing bridge and tending roses in public gardens.

Cletus Capitano is a teacher.

Linda Conti received a degree in Communication Arts and worked on both the West and East Coasts as a marketing and public relations professional in higher education for over 35 years. She continues to provide freelance marketing and web design services, but has now dedicated most of her professional endeavors to fiction writing and photography. "Sweetie Pie and the other Colorful Birds in Mrs. Bumberly's Backyard" is her first photo-illustrated children's book. To view her photography, order a photo-illustrated book of "Sweetie Pie," or to purchase bird memorabilia, go to: http://www.abirdslife.org or email info@abirdslife.org.

R. David Drucker's mother predicted, although he could barely have known at the time, that he would become a priest or a comedian. As an adult, he split the difference and became a poet. Drucker is a trained anthropologist/archaeologist/ethnohistorian with field experience in Central Mexico and New York State. Drucker was also a classical music announcer on the still lamented WBFB [a.k.a. WBBF-FM] in Rochester, NY, taught anthropology at SUNY Geneseo, worked as a radiocarbon technician at Krueger Enterprises, Cambridge MA, was Museum Manager for Shako:wi Cultural Center in Oneida, NY, and Museum Director for the Chenango County Historical Society Museum in Norwich, NY.

Drucker had been writing verse for many decades, but the shock of the sudden death of his wife of 32 years, Mary, on January 14, 2015 transfigured him into a poet. Three other deaths of people deeply significant to him followed during the next two years. The stimulus of these four intense periods of grief awakened other feelings and memories in him. A return to a love of Mexico, sailing and the sea, and Buddhist philosophy began to spring spontaneously onto the page as a result. Drucker immodestly characterizes his writing process as Mozartean - spontaneous and rapid thanks to technique so overlearned as to be unconscious, chiefly the unwavering use of ten syllable lines in his work. He has been writing at least one poem a day for the past three years. He is a regular reader at the monthly poetry HOOT at Café Espresso, Portsmouth, NH.

Besides his daily writing discipline, Drucker volunteers as a UNH Marine Docent, a crewmember of the replica gundalow "Piscataqua," a Hospice client visitor, and a South Church Board of Trustees member. Drucker's love of music from childhood is fed by his participation in various choirs and singing groups on the New Hampshire Seacoast and in nearby Southern Maine. He resides in Dover, NH.

Royaline Edwards dedicated herself to the nurturing of young minds for 34 years as an elementary teacher in Kittery, Maine, and Portsmouth, New Hampshire. Retiring in 1999, she continued her presence in education as an Artist in Residence in various schools on the New Hampshire Seacoast, working with teachers and students in the presentation of an original play, *Listen to the Drums–A Tribute to Harriet Tubman*. Between productions of "Drums" she worked as a guest teacher in Kittery and Eliot, Maine for the past 18 years.

The Artist in Residence Program was expanded to include a local theater in Portsmouth. Seeking a wider venue to bring the message of her play to the community, Royaline was asked by a theater representative if it could be presented during Black History month. After overcoming some obstacles, a cast was assembled from former "Drum" actors as well as from youth in the Seacoast Repertory Theater and other community organizations.

Royaline's love for reading and writing goes back to her childhood. It was not until years later, as a first grade teacher, she became serious enough about her writing to enroll in a course at the Institute of Children's Literature, in West Redding, Connecticut, followed by her enrollment in their *Revise to Publish Workshop.* Her first book, *A Ribbon for Sammi,* was published in 2009. Since that time, her long-time courtship with writing was sparked anew after enrolling in the local course, *Writing for Children and Young Adults.* She plans to launch her second book, *Kandi,* in the near future.

She is married to Kelvin C. Edwards and together they have two grown children, Trent and Alysa. Both are married with five children between them: Langston, Landon, Raina and Alfred Jenkins III, and Dylan Edwards.

Roland Goodbody grew up on the Hampshire-West Sussex border in the sweep of the South Downs, a National Park in England, where his family still lives. After earning a B.A. at the University of Keele and briefly teaching English in Spain, he moved to New Hampshire in 1976. He worked for thirty-three years at the University of New Hampshire, first at the bookstore, and then in the library, where he eventually became an archivist for over 20 years. He is also an actor and theatre director, and a former radio deejay, having hosted "Ceili," a Celtic music show on WUNH for 26 years.

Kate Johnston was born on Cape Cod, and raised in rural New Hampshire where nature and wildlife stirred her imagination. She knew she wanted to be a professional writer when she was about 8 years old and wrote a story about a good wolf. Married with two children, Kate likes to spend her mornings writing YA and Adult fiction. Her work can be found in *Compass Points: Stories from Seacoast Authors, The Greensilk Journal, Wolf Warriors, Northeast Wolf Coalition,* and her blog on living as a writer, katejohnstonauthor.com.

A story coach, Kate inspires writers to take their creativity to the next level so they can write successfully with confidence, joy, and rumbling creativity. She also teaches creative writing to kids in after-school enrichment programs and is currently organizing a fundraising book project called *Dare to be a Voice,* featuring her local students' short stories that focus on conservation issues.

When she's not writing, Kate loves to spend time with her family and pets, explore nature, watch Disney films, and bake ooey-gooey desserts. And purposely write fragments.

Susan McCarthy lives with her family in Southern Maine.

Liz Newman has traveled a long and winding road to arrive at her proper place in her life. After working in finance for 15 years and earning a Master's degree in Economics, she returned to school to follow her passion and earned a Bachelor's degree in Fine Arts from the Fiber Arts Department at Massachusetts College of Art. She decided to try her hand at writing and found it to be an even better outlet for her creativity than her visual art. She now works as an assistant to a fiber artist in Boston, MA, a pet sitter / dog walker in New Hampshire and Maine and boards dogs in her home. She lives in Kittery, Maine with her husband, 2 dogs and 3 cats.

Elizabeth Kilcoyne has just begun to write for herself and loves it! In her career, Elizabeth focused on technical and policy writing which came easily. The description and action and emotion in her new stories are challenging for her. She follows an Arthur Ashe approach to life: "Start where you are, use what you have, do what you can." Elizabeth lives with her husband in Newburyport, MA.

Luke Pettis earned a Bachelor's Degree in Creative Writing from New England College in 2017. He is now applying his writing skills by creating newspaper articles, website content, and fiction. He one day hopes to create his own fantasy series to share with the world. He lives in Dover, NH with his family and his cat Blizzard.

Karina Quintans is a self-employed technical writer based in Portsmouth, New Hampshire. A third culture kid, she was born in Boston to Filipino parents, and raised in the Middle East, South America, Europe. She has continued to travel around the world for work and pleasure. In addition to writing, Karina is passionate about photography. In her free time, she enjoys hiking, craft beer, spending time with family, and being civically engaged. Karina holds an undergraduate degree in Finance, and a graduate degree in International Development.

Woody Sponaugle lives in Rye, NH where, for the past nine years, he has been a full-time caregiver for his wife who has Alzheimer's. Previously, over the past 50 years, he had been a business owner, entrepreneur, turnaround manager, consultant and attorney. He has managed businesses and projects in a variety of industries and countries including the US, Thailand, China, Slovakia, Saudi Arabia, Egypt, and Russia. Originally from Lancaster PA, he received a BA in Government from Cornell Univ.; a JD from Vanderbilt University Law School, and attended Executive Education Programs at Harvard Business School and Dartmouth's Tuck School of Business.

A. Rebecca Wagner has been in love with the written word since third grade. She has been an avid attendee of writing workshops and classes since the age of 12. She is constantly retreating to fictional places, filling notebooks with tales of childhood adventures in her second hometown of Merrimac, Massachusetts. She has also proudly completed a trilogy, *The Wolf Creek Alternative School Chronicles*, loosely based on her high school years at Coastal Alternative School in Salisbury, Massachusetts. Currently residing in Dover, New Hampshire, she is hard at work on the continuation of Ember's story and traveling the road of life with her husband, twelve year old son, and Thoreau the hermit crab. She strives to get lost in unfamiliar places, loves the escape of great music and reveres long walks, especially after dark when the world is quiet. She is in search of an agent to help make her dream of the writing life a reality.

35699846R00131

Made in the USA
Columbia, SC
22 November 2018